"Ayden's Awakening"

By

Justus Roux

Also by Justus Roux

My Master
Master's Ecstasy
Obey!
Sweet Rapture
Mistress Angelique
Wrath's Lust
Erotic Moments
Protector of My Heart
Keeper of My Soul
Heavenly Surrender
Breathless

Edited by Justus Roux
Erotic Tales
Erotic Fantasy: Tales of the Paranormal

Cover art by Marketing Edge Designs
http://marketingedgedesigns.com/

ISBN 0-9754080-6-2

This book is dedicated to my family who has listened to me prattle on about my hunters. I have really enjoyed writing this series of books and to have you guys enjoy being my sounding board as I plotted out each part of this series means more to me than mere words can express. Thank you for always being there for me.

Ayden could feel her, see her, he could almost smell her. But he was afraid to go to her. She had dominated his thoughts from the moment he learned of her existence. He has only shown his love for her in her dreams. He ached to touch her. He longed to know what her lips taste like. He tries to deny the bond that is growing between them. He tries to keep his distance, but he is drawn to her.

He remembered that moment when the image of her filled his mind. He was alone after he had brought Jasmine and Ryo's souls back from Purgatory. His lonely soul called out and she answered. Just like the others before, but this time it felt different and it scared him. He had waited centuries for this moment and now he was afraid of what his love might do to his... soul mate. Was that what she was, his soul mate?

"Emily..." he whispered her name and warmth filled his body.

Now Emily's life was in danger. Lasax's anger would not be sated until Emily was hunted down. But if Ayden revealed himself to her...he didn't know what to do. The only thing he knew is that he loves her. Even though he has never held her in reality, he loves her and nothing, not even Lasax would harm her. Not as long as there was breath left in his body.

Chapter 1

Emily entered the shower and let the warm water run down her body. Today her divorce was final. She was neither sad nor happy. After all, Scott did leave her six months ago. She had plenty of time to grieve the loss of her marriage. She cupped her full breasts in her hands. The weight of them in her hands reminded her of the twenty pounds she had to lose yet. Scott's new girlfriend didn't have such worries. Emily quickly let her mind think of something else. Her self-esteem was low enough already, no need punishing herself.

Yet, even with her life turned upside down, she couldn't help but smile. At least her dream world was active. The man she created to star in them was amazing looking. His golden hair and eyes, warm smile, soothing voice and perfect body filled her thoughts. She had to give herself credit, if she was going to fantasize at least her mind thought up something really good. "Ayden," she chuckled. She even gave her fantasy man a name.

She climbed out of the shower and dried herself off. Today she was moving into her new apartment. She and Scott agreed to sell the house, not like she wanted to live in a place with so many memories anyways.

She wiped the fog off the mirror and looked at herself. "Well girl today you are officially a single woman again." She should be more upset, but she wasn't. "Enough of this." She hurried to finish getting ready,

Shelly and Diane would be here soon to help her move into her apartment and new life.

As she dressed her mind kept going back to Ayden. Lately, she thought about him a lot. She knew it was kind of weird to be daydreaming about a dream, but still she found Ayden's image constantly in her mind. Some days she couldn't wait to go to sleep and slip into her fantasy world to be with him. She was sure a shrink would say she was escaping the harsh reality of her divorce and this is how she coped. In truth however she started to believe that maybe Scott leaving her wasn't a bad thing that in fact it might have been just what she needed. Or maybe even this line of thinking was her way to cope.

She pulled back her long dark hair. Today was going to be a very busy one. She looked around at all the boxes. She packed all this stuff through the week. She got rid of a lot of things that she and Scott shared. All that was left was things that belonged only to her.

Shelly and Diane have been so wonderful through all of this. They were more like sisters than friends. They were always there for her ever since high school. The three musketeers as Diane loved to call them. Right now she was grateful she had such close friends.

Emily walked over to the window and looked at the U-haul truck that was sitting in the driveway then she turned from the window and looked over what she could of the house. "Well, it's over, seven years of marriage and two years of dating over." Her life had changed in an instant and she had a strange feeling that this was only the tip of the iceberg.

೫೦೫೦೫೦

Ayden closed his eyes and pictured Emily. She was so beautiful to him. He could see her so clearly in his mind.

She was rather petite, had long brown hair and warm brown eyes. Her smile was amazing. Her soft curves made his hands ache to caress her. Her soul was so loving, she could find good in almost anything. This inner beauty radiated out and made her glow.

However, he was afraid. What if his love destroyed her beautiful soul? Could he risk her like that? His body ached for hers. His arms long to embrace her. Never had he felt so connected to any other woman. Was Emily his salvation? Did he dare to hope? It was his fear of destroying her that kept him from finding her.

He had visited her in her dreams. She was so open to him. But then again he was only in her dream. Her heart had been wounded recently and he wanted to bring her comfort. How could any man let such a woman as Emily go?

If she were here with him, he would show her how love was suppose to feel. But...Ayden was afraid...

"Ayden," Gabriele's voice brought him back to reality.

"What is it Gabriele?"

"Have you found Emily yet?"

"No."

Gabriele squatted down so she could look Ayden in the eyes. "Asurul said we have to find her quickly."

"I know."

"Then focus."

"I will find her Gabriele." Ayden could understand Gabriele's frustration. But how could she possibly understand his fear. No one could. Not one of his demon hunters could possibly understand the pain of watching a woman destroy herself simply because he chose to love her. He just didn't know if he could risk that with Emily.

"Ayden, you have to find her. Even if you don't wish to reveal yourself to her, we have to protect her."

"You are right Gabriele." Ayden closed his eyes again and focused on Emily. He had to find her. His hunters would be able to protect her and he would protect her even if he couldn't be with her.

"Ayden"

Ayden's eyes popped open upon hearing Emily's sweet voice in his mind. She called out to him, she never done that before. He usually went to her.

"What is wrong?" Gabriele asked.

"Nothing," Ayden almost growled. He stood up and walked away from Gabriele. He had to have a moment alone. However, finding this moment would prove difficult, his hunters always were there. He cared deeply for each one of them but at times their constant presence grew irritating.

"Hey Gabriele, give Ayden a few moments alone."

Ayden sighed with relief upon hearing Ryker's voice. He knew Gabriele would listen to her soul mate. Ryker though mortal was a pleasant change. He didn't treat Ayden like a priceless treasure in constant need of guarding. Once Ryker got use to Ayden's presence he treated him just like any other comrade, a fact in which Ayden was most grateful.

Ayden walked out into the forest. They were getting ready to leave the hunting cabins to find Emily. The nearest Ayden could tell she was in an average size town in Washington.

These cabins, every time Ayden looked at them they reminded him of his weakness. Ryo and Jasmine almost lost their lives because of him. It was only Ryo's love for Jasmine that saved them. That moment he saw Ryo and Jasmine's souls reaching, that moment still frightened him. Even his mother Isa couldn't explain how he was able to see their souls.

Ayden leaned up against the tree. There were so many questions he needed answers to. But Emily was the only thing he could think of. He closed his eyes and focused on her. The vision of her was fuzzy she must not be asleep. His bond with her was strong. Though he has loved and lost many women over the hundreds of years he was alive, none of them felt like this. Images of his past lovers flooded his mind. Suicides, murders, and mental homes, the ugliness of it all was almost unbearable. Each woman wanting to own him, to control him, and he tried to give each what they needed. But soon their jealousy would consume them. He didn't want this for Emily. He toyed with the idea of giving himself over to Lasax or Prolo. This would ensure Emily's safety. But then he would think of the great sacrifices previous demon hunters had made, giving their lives to protect him. The struggle his parents went through to ensure his safety. He couldn't just let their sacrifices be in vain.

"Damn it !!" Ayden cried out. The woman he has been searching for was within his reach and his damn fear kept him from reaching out to her.

"Ayden"

"Emily…" Ayden slid down the tree until he was sitting on the ground. He closed his eyes and focused with everything he had. She needed him.

"If only you were real Ayden." He could see her unpacking treasured items and the tears in her eyes.

"I am real Emily," he cried out. Her pain raked through him. If only he could hold her and kiss away those tears before they stained her beautiful face.

"Ayden."

He looked up when he felt the gentle touch of his mother. "Mother, I don't know what to do."

"You will." She sat down next to him. That look of anguish on his face tore at her. "You must find her. I feel that her life is in danger." She reached up and stroked his hair. "I don't say this lightly my son. You must find her. Now try to concentrate on her."

Ayden felt his mother leave as he focused all his energy on Emily. He would have to set aside his fear of destroying her in order to save her. Ayden almost laughed at the irony of his situation.

Chapter 2

"AHHH!" Lasax screamed. All of Hell trembled. "Get in here you worthless Generals." Soon the room filled with men and women. "I sent my best Generals out to kill Ayden and still he lives. Damn them." Lasax grabbed the nearest General and turned her into a pile of ash. "Manus, at least battled with Ayden." Every time Lasax would move the herd of men and women would back away from him. "I will not let that son of a traitor be my equal!" His voice boomed across the room, never had any of the Generals seen Lasax so angry.

"Master," a tall well-muscled man spoke up.

"Tryton, choose your words carefully."

"I have a suggestion." Tryton didn't budge when Lasax charged at him.

"Really…" Lasax picked Tryton up by the neck and lifted him off the ground.

"Kill me if you must Master." Tryton locked eyes with Lasax. Asurul had taught him not to ever show fear to Lasax, for that was the one thing Lasax despised. This was one of the many lessons the great General Asurul taught him.

Amused by Tryton's courage he let him go. "Tell me your suggestion."

Tryton rubbed his neck. "Kill the woman named Emily. You said you believe she is Ayden's soul mate. But don't stop there Master, kill all the mortal soul mates of Asurul's hunters. For a man or woman without the other half of their soul is an easy opponent to defeat."

Lasax started to laugh. "Very good Tryton." Lasax ran his fingers through Tryton's long blond hair. "Asurul is forbidden to aid Ayden. I will see to it that Asurul is confined to his paradise. This will ensure he doesn't aid those damn hunters."

"What of Prolo, Master?" a beautiful woman with dark hair and eyes spoke up.

"Come Evity."

She went right to him. Though afraid of what he might do to her, even she knew it was foolish to show fear before Lasax.

"I will deal with Prolo. But, you are wise to consider the threat he may cause." Lasax turned to the rest. "I am appointing Tryton, Grand General, and Evity second in command. I will be sending quite a few of you worthless Generals up to Earth and you will obey Tryton and Evity."

"Yes Master," they said in unison.

"Then go, kill this Emily and every one of those hunters' soul mates as well. Then I will witness the end of the son of Asurul. Fail me this time and all of you will know just how bad I can make Hell." Lasax watched his Generals leave the room. With so many of them going up to Earth Prolo would surely send his damn Archangels down. This didn't concern Lasax, how hard was it to kill a bunch of mortals. Oh, the delicious despair he would feel coming from Ayden and those damn demon hunters once their lovers were dead, mmmm, Lasax became very aroused by the mere thought. He reached out and grabbed two beautiful women. He always kept some of his Generals around for this purpose. His lust was insatiable.

"What is your pleasure Master," one woman purred.

"You lay down and you wait. I will need to fuck both of you to sate me."

Lasax grabbed the golden hair woman's hips and pulled her to him. He impaled her, driving his enormous cock as deep as it could go. He growled and grunted as he rammed his cock in and out, not caring whether he was harming the woman or not. His hands tore into her flesh as he thrust harder and faster. "Come here," he growled, pulling the other woman to him. He pulled his cock out of the blonde-haired woman then forced the red-haired one to her hands and knees. With one forceful thrust he filled her full of his cock. He continued switching between the two women until blood ran down their thighs. Finally as he rode the blonde for the tenth time his orgasm started to build. He thrust frantically needing release. As he came the blonde screamed out in agony, his cum burnt every inch of her flesh it touched.

Lasax pushed the women out of his bed. His thoughts were on Tryton and Evity they better bring him Ayden this time. The Creator just informed him of his plans for Ayden and each time Lasax thought about it, the more he seethed.

ജ്ജ

"Master." Tasmos quickly entered Prolo's chambers.

"What is it Tasmos?" Prolo sat up in his bed. He gently removed the woman who was busy sucking on his cock and shooed away the man who was caressing his shoulders.

"Lasax has released several Generals." Tasmos stepped back as Prolo climbed out of the bed.

"Are you certain?" Prolo stood still as the woman wrapped a white silken cloth around his waist.

"Yes Master."

"What are you up to Lasax? Tasmos follow me." Prolo headed out of the room then down the hall to his crystal pond. He waved his hand over it and images of

Earth flashed. He witness demon Generals one after the other emerging from the ground.

"Tasmos ready a squadron of your finest Archangels."

"Yes Master." Tasmos hurried from the room.

"Creator, do you not see what Lasax is doing?" Prolo shouted out.

"I do Prolo," a voice neither man nor woman answered.

"Then forgive me for saying this, but why are you allowing him to do this?"

"Ayden has found his soul mate, as too has all his hunters that were meant to find theirs."

"I don't understand."

"Ayden is being tested."

"For what, Creator?"

"Necoblas has grown weary and has turned Purgatory into a wasteland."

"Forgive me but I still don't understand."

"Necoblas no longer wishes to rule Purgatory. Ayden will take his place."

"What!?" Prolo clenched his fist. "That son of those two traitors will be the ruler of Purgatory. This can't be."

"You dare to question my judgment?"

"Of course not, but…"

"Necoblas was once a great leader but his loneliness consumed him, thus causing Purgatory to turn into what it is now. This was not meant to be this way."

Prolo backed up when a lighted figure descended from the ceiling. "When a soul's mortal body dies that soul is frightened, not all souls deserve the misery Necoblas forces them to endure." Prolo came to his knees and lowered his head. "Ayden will bring the warmth back to Purgatory; he will restore it to what it was meant to be."

"Surely there is someone more worthy than Ayden."

"Who better than Ayden, he is part angel, demon and human."

Prolo felt a warmth flood his body. He gazed up and a woman with beauty beyond compare gazed down at him. "Prolo do what is in your heart to do. You and Lasax will test Ayden."

"If he fails?"

"Then Necoblas will have to wait until another worthy soul is born."

"Thank you Creator."

Prolo felt the warmth leave him and he knew the Creator had gone. "Damn it, if I knew that was Ayden's purpose, I would have sent my Archangels to kill him long ago." Prolo went back to the pond and waved his hand over it. The image of Lasax appeared before him. He could see the rage in Lasax's eyes. If Lasax was sending so many Generals then he too knew of Ayden's fate.

Prolo stood up and waved his hand again, clearing the pond. For now he would worry about clearing out some of those demons. Too many on Earth would only tempt the beasts to quench their need for mayhem. This would be counter productive to the main goal.

"Tasmos!" Prolo yelled.

"Yes Master."

"Is your squadron ready?"

"Yes Master."

"For now kill only the demons that harm innocent mortals. We can't have them making a bloody mess down there."

"Yes Master." With that, Tasmos left.

Prolo walked back to his chamber. He had much to decide. If Lasax was so upset about this news, maybe Ayden being the leader of Purgatory wasn't such a bad thing. However, Prolo's pride wouldn't let him allow it.

Chapter 3

Emily carefully placed the figurines on the shelf. Scott bought her each one of these little dragons. She always had a thing about dragons. Scott knew this and always made sure to have some sort of dragon image in the gifts he gave her. Strange, she thought she put the tears behind her. But looking at these beautiful dragons she felt the familiar pain come back. She and Scott were married for seven years. She believed they were happy, up until six months ago when he announced he was leaving her. He handed her the divorce papers right then and there. No sorrow, no regret, no anything in his eyes. He just wanted to be rid of her and their life together. How can someone claim to love you one minute then just stop?

"Enough of this." She wiped the tears away. Crying wasn't going to make him come back and to be honest she didn't know if she would take him back. She stood up and walked over to another box. Shelly and Diane were busy unpacking all the kitchen stuff and left Emily alone to unpack the bedroom things. Emily smiled she loved her friends they seem to know just what she needed. She didn't know if she could have gotten through all of this without them.

"This is so tiring," Emily said as she went over to the bed. She lay down and just looked up at the ceiling. She gasped when thoughts of Ayden bombarded her mind. "You will have to wait until I go to sleep Ayden," she chuckled.

"Emily..."

His deep, sexy voice aroused her. Her little fantasy thing was starting to get out of hand. It's one thing to have Mr. Perfect in her dreams, but hearing his voice while she was awake, now that was different. Oh Ayden was perfect too. She closed her eyes and indulged herself. Her hands reached out to touch his sculpted chest in her mind while outside her daydream her hand went down to her pussy.

"Emily," he sighed as her hands caressed his chest.

Emily let her hands wander down his body as her fingers caressed her clit. She watched as he slowly removed his pants. She licked her lips in anticipation as his beautiful cock was slowly revealed to her. She imagined her hand wrapping around the shaft as her eyes stayed focused on his gorgeous face. She slowly stroked up and down his cock watching the look of pleasure on his face. Her fingers circled faster and faster on her clit. Her body shuddered when he moaned.

"Ayden, if only you were real," she sighed.

"I am real Emily."

"No your not, you are just a wonderful figment of my imagination."

"I am very real."

Emily sat up. "Oh great, now my fantasy man is going to argue with me." She decided now probably wasn't the best time to pleasure herself anyways. She wouldn't want to embarrass her friends should they walk in on her.

"I am real, Emily, and I am coming for you."

Emily just stood there for a moment. She felt someone gently caressing her body and it frightened her. Ayden sensed her fear and immediately stopped.

"Shelly, Diane, I am coming to help you guys for awhile." She took one last look over the bedroom. No, Ayden didn't just caress her, no, no, it must be her imagination. She convinced herself of this and hurried downstairs to help the others.

ഇ෩ഇ෩ഇ෩

Ayden's cock was so hard it ached. He reached back down and slowly began stroking his cock again. He closed his eyes and pictured Emily. He pictured her lying under him with her beautiful legs wrapped around his waist. His hand slid faster and faster up and down his cock as he tried to imagine what it would feel like having his cock buried deeply in her. "Emily," he sighed as he reached up his hand and grabbed the tree he was leaning against. He tilted his head back as he orgasm, his hand slowly stroked milking every last drop of his cum out. "Emily," he whispered as he enjoyed the afterglow of his climax.

His moment of serenity was brief as a feeling of dread washed over him.

"I must go to her." Ayden stood up and straightened himself up before he walked back towards the hunting cabins. He could feel the presence of several demon Generals. This was most disturbing, never had he felt the presence of so many Generals before. He hurried over towards his hunters.

Ryo had his sword drawn. "Do you feel their presence?" Ryo asked.

"Yes, prepare to leave this area," Ayden answered. He watched Gabriele pack up their weapons and supplies. Saban was heading towards Ryker. Ayden almost chuckled when Ryker backed away from Saban protesting that he didn't want to be carried by him. Ryo already had Jasmine scooped up in his arms.

"I told Michael and Miranda where to meet you," Isa said, grabbing Ayden's hand. "You must go to Emily. She needs your protection."

"I will protect her, mother. I will worry about my feelings for her later."

Before Isa could reply she was torn away from Ayden. "Mother!" Ayden reached for her just before she disappeared.

"Mommy and Daddy can't help you or your hunters, Ayden." Lasax's voice boomed in his mind.

"I don't need their help to defeat your pathetic army!" Ayden shouted out. The others just looked at him, not knowing who he was talking to.

"Are you all right?" Gabriele asked as she threw the weapons pack over her shoulder.

"Yes, Asurul will not be aiding any of you. We are alone and I fear Lasax and Prolo will try their best to destroy me this time."

"Not with us around they won't," Gabriele said.

"I have faith in all of your abilities." Ayden waited for them to get ready. He could fly like an Archangel, but he opted just to use his demon speed, so his hunters would be able to keep up with him.

"Oh no..." Ryker groaned when Saban picked him up and threw him over his shoulder. "I really hate this stuff, Gabriele."

"So do I Ryker," Jasmine added as she latched onto Ryo.

Ayden started to laugh then he raced off. The others were right behind him.

Chapter 4

Tryton emerged from the ground. He shook the dirt off him and then quickly killed all the lesser-demons who tried to emerge. "I don't need you pest getting in the way," he said as he sliced the last one. He positioned the demon Generals in various locations then sent them on their way. This should keep Prolo's Archangels busy. He knew his fellow demons, they wouldn't resist the urge to play with the mortals who were unlucky enough to cross their path.

"You are allowing me to stay with you?" Alma asked. She adored Tryton, but he looked at her as though she was just some pest, though he seemed to keep her by his side, giving her hope that he might hold one small spark of affection for her.

"I will need to be amused." He chuckled. Torturing her brought him much delight.

"I can think of several ways to amuse you." Alma closed the distance between them.

"Really?" Tryton smiled.

"I want you," she purred as she ran her hands over his hard, sculpted chest.

"Mmm, how much do you want me?" He slowly let his tongue wet his lips, knowing she was watching every movement he made. He could see the lust in her eyes.

"More than you can imagine."

"So, if I told you to beg for my cock, you would do it?"

"If it pleases you."

"Then beg." Tryton smacked her hand away from his crotch. "Ah, ah, beg me."

"Please Tryton fuck me, oh use me. I will do anything you say. Please."

"No." He pushed her away.

"You bastard," she hissed at him.

Tryton laughed loudly. He so loved messing with her, but there was no way he would stick his cock into that worthless demon bitch. If she had any dignity she would push him away, like Kali used to do. Now that was a woman worthy of him. Too bad Kali fell in love with an Archangel and got herself killed. Well at least Evity was still here. He admired her, she was strong and intelligent. This couldn't be said for Alma.

"You two come here." He pointed at two young, pretty looking male demons.

"Yes Tryton," they both said behind gritted teeth. The mere thought of taking orders from anyone other than Lasax bugged the hell out of both of them. After all they were Generals too.

"I can feel your distain for me and quite frankly I don't give a shit what you think." Tryton pointed out towards the west. "There is a small town not more than twenty miles ahead. Go find this woman named Emily Jacobs and bring her to me.

"Why don't you do this yourself?"

"I have to set a trap for Ayden's hunters, now go and don't question my orders again." Trying to get all these fledgling demons to work together was going to be a real pain in the ass. However, they were mostly fodder for those Archangels. The more skilled demons were being saved back for the main plan.

"Come Alma, let's go find some mortals to play with." Tryton turned to her and smiled at the eagerness in her eyes. "If you are a good little demon bitch I will let you watch me."

Alma could feel the shame and lust combine as she saw that smug look on his face. She knew she would do whatever he asked. This both repulsed and excited her. She followed him like the obedient slave she was.

ഇരു ഇരു ഇരു

"Oh damn that looks good," Shelly said, grabbing a piece of pizza.

"Yes it does," Diane added.

Emily set out the napkins then joined her friends at the small kitchen table. "Thanks you guys." She raised her diet soda up to toast. "To a fresh start."

"Fresh start," the others joined in.

"You know this place is rather cute and cozy," Diane said as she ate the pizza.

"I like it." Emily looked around. It was a rather quaint little apartment.

The women finished their meal while they discussed Emily's future. After a bit, Emily escorted the women to the door. "Thanks again." They were so sweet to help her move into her new apartment. Having their company helped ease this transition.

"You sure you don't want us to spend the night?" Shelly asked

"No, it's better if I spend this first night alone."

"Well you know what's best for you. Call us if you change your mind." Diane gave her a big hug, so too did Shelley.

"Bye guys." Emily waited until they were in their car before she closed the door. The silence was strange, but yet welcoming. She cleaned up the table then headed into the living room. She plopped down on the sofa and took a deep breath in.

"Now what?" she sighed. Her whole life was so mapped out, until six months ago. She looked over at the box with her art supplies. It had been ages since she drew or painted anything. She made a mental note to pick out a nice spot to set up her easel.

"Why not," she said as she went over to the box and took out her sketchpad and drawing pencils. She went back over to the sofa and sat down. She thought for a moment then started sketching. Slowly an image of a man appeared as she continued to draw. "Ayden." She smiled. She was amazed at the detail she was able to put into her sketch. She spent extra attention on his beautiful eyes, so warm, so alive. The golden color of his eyes danced in her mind, though she couldn't capture the brilliance of the color in just a black and white sketch. She drew only his face and shoulders then framed his face with his long, lush, golden hair. She remembered how the highlights in his golden hair sparkled. She would have to paint this picture, she thought to herself.

After an hour she finished her sketch. She ran her fingers over his lush lips. "I have been dreaming about you too long, Ayden," she said as she set her sketchpad down on the sofa. She reclined back she was starting to get tired. It had been a long day and she was drained physically as well as mentally.

"Emily…"

She sat straight up when she heard Ayden's voice. There was a strange urgency to his tone. She felt a panic start to build, but from what she didn't know.

Her eyes darted up to the ceiling when she heard a strange scurrying noise. "That's a big mouse." She slowly came to her feet. That almost sounded like a person walking on the roof. But, that can't be. Her apartment was on the fourth floor.

"Emily stay where you are."

"Ayden?" She looked around the room. She was still alone. She couldn't be hearing his voice in her head. That wasn't possible.

A loud crashing sound came from the bedroom. She slowly went into the kitchen and grabbed a large chef's knife. Oh shit, someone was breaking into her apartment. There was no time to call anyone. If she tried to leave whoever it was would surely hear her.

"I smell a mortal's pussy, here pussy, pussy, pussy."

Emily tightened her grip on the knife's handle "Who are you?" she shouted when she saw the silhouette of a man.

"Julius." The man moved closer, as he did Emily could start to make out his features. He was well-muscled, with dark hair, he was rather handsome, but there was no beauty in his eyes, only hate.

"What do you want?"

"Your pussy."

Emily backed away. There was no way she could stop this man from hurting her. She held the knife so tightly her hand began to ache.

"Your fear is turning me on."

"Julius stop fucking around and grab the little bitch."

Emily gasped when another man who looked exactly like the first one entered the kitchen. He moved Julius aside and headed for her.

"It seems she is the one everyone is searching for." Marcus held up Emily's sketchpad for Julius to see.

"I will be damned... hey wait I already am damned." Julius chuckled.

"Very nice likeness to that bastard Ayden," Marcus said as he tore the drawing out of the pad then proceeded to rip it up. "Now I will take this woman to Tryton …"

"Back off Marcus, I will take her to Tryton." The two men got into a shoving match.

"Emily run!!"

Without thinking Emily dropped the knife and raced for the door. She flung it open then ran as fast as she could to the stairs. She hurried down the stairs. She heard the men's laughter as they followed her. She pushed opened the door that led outside and ran across the pavement.

"No!!!" She heard Julius scream out.

She didn't look behind her, she just ran. She felt something impact with her then her feet leaving the ground. She looked down and watched the ground getting further and further away from her feet. She reached down and felt a man's strong arm around her.

"You are safe now."

"Ayden?" She tried to look behind her but he held her so tightly she couldn't move.

"Yes, it's me. Please be calm." Ayden could feel her fear and confusion and it tore at him. He wished there was another way to slowly tell her what was going on, but he didn't have the luxury to do that. He had to get her away from those two deviant demons.

"Calm!" Emily closed her eyes.

"Please trust me." Ayden landed then escorted Emily toward Michael. "My soul is in your hands, Michael."

"Nothing will harm her." Michael gently grabbed Emily.

Emily could only watch as Ayden flew away. "He is flying. How is that possible?"

"It's okay." Miranda took Emily's hand.

"The hell it is. Nobody can fly." Emily looked around. A tall, gorgeous, blond- haired man was standing next to her. She looked into the petite dark-haired woman's beautiful green eyes. "What is going on?"

"My name is Miranda and this is my husband Michael. We are here to help you."

"Help me?" Emily's eyes darted everywhere. They were in some kind of park. "Who were those two men?"

"I know you are scared. Everything will be explained, but first we must get you to safety."

Emily didn't know what to think. That man who just flew away couldn't have been Ayden, after all Ayden was only a fantasy she dreamt up, not to mention he flew away. Emily's breath started to come in short bursts. What was going on? She felt Miranda rubbing her back and telling her to take deep breaths.

"Michael." Miranda looked up at him.

"Please Emily come with me."

Before Emily could reply Michael had already picked her up. He had her in one arm and Miranda in the other.

"Hold on tight, Emily," Miranda said as she held onto Michael's arm. Emily did what she said.

"Holy shit!" Emily exclaimed when Michael started running. Not only did he hold on to her with only one arm, not to mention holding the other woman with his other arm, he also was running so fast that everything that past was a blur. Emily closed her eyes and held on to his arm tight. She didn't know what the hell was happening, but somehow she knew she was safe, for now anyways. It was almost as if someone else was sending her waves of reassurance, letting her know she was safe.

෨෨෨

Ryo watched as Ayden destroyed Julius and Marcus. Never had he seen Ayden kill with such hatred before. Ryker and Jasmine were with Saban, away from all of this. But still he felt nervous not being near Jasmine. There were too many demon Generals out there. He glanced over to Gabriele and could tell by the expression on her face she felt the same way about leaving Ryker's side.

"We must search the area to be sure those two were the only Generals in this area. I feel the presence of at least one more," Ayden said as he approached the two.

"We will check the area, you should go to Emily," Gabriele said.

"I will help you."

"Ayden, Gabriele is right. Michael may need help. This seems too organized. I fear it might be some sort of trap," Ryo added.

Ayden couldn't deny the truth in Ryo's words. This did feel like some sort of trap, but for whom. "Go back to your soul mates. We will then regroup and begin our hunt." Ayden took to the sky.

Ryo and Gabriele hurried off. They didn't want to chance their soul mates safety. Something was wrong. The sooner they regroup the better.

Emily was here with him now and he didn't know what to do. Ayden scanned the area as he flew across the sky towards Emily. He sent her reassurance hoping to at least bring her a measure of calm. When he felt those two demons so close to her, he had to get to her, he cursed himself for his fear. He almost lost her because he took so long to find her. Having her briefly in his arms felt so right, the warmth of her smaller body next to his and her scent lingered with him. Her confusion and fear enveloped him, feeling as though someone punched him in the stomach. He had to hurry and get to her, but once he was there what was he going to say or do?

Chapter 5

Michael gently let Emily go. She immediately sat down. Her stomach was queasy and her head spun. Emily looked up and saw the group of people standing around her. There were two women and three men. She couldn't make out what they were saying, but they kept looking down at her as though she was a valuable archeological find or something. What the hell was going on? Was this some bizarre dream? Was she dead? Her breathing started to pick up pace and she fought back her tears.

"Where is Ayden?" Saban asked as he looked down at Emily. She looked so frightened and confused. Ayden should be here to comfort her.

"He is on his way, along with Ryo and Gabriele," Michael replied.

Jasmine walked over to Emily. She knew what Emily must feel like. She too, was in a very similar situation herself, when Ryo came for her. She glanced up at Ryker and Miranda and could tell they also felt empathy for Emily.

"It's okay," Jasmine said, sitting down next to Emily.

"Tell me what's going on."

"Ayden should be the one who explains everything to you."

"Ayden..." Emily stood up. "Ayden is just someone I made up in my dreams."

Jasmine grabbed Emily's hand, she felt so sorry for the poor thing.

"I am real Emily." Ayden walked slowly over to her. He wanted so much to take her into his arms and bring some measure of comfort to her. His body almost trembled being so near to her.

Emily spun around and then just stood there in shock. There was the man of her dreams standing not more than a few feet ahead of her. Her eyes slowly traveled up his beautiful body. The only thing he wore was a pair of jeans. He had just taken off his tattered shirt, remnants of his last battle. His golden hair hung down past his shoulders like a curtain of silk. Her eyes journeyed up to his full sensuous lips. His face was sheer male perfection. Her eyes locked with his golden colored eyes. There was such warmth in his gaze she was in danger of getting lost in it.

"This can't be." Her eyes couldn't leave him.

"I know you are frightened." Ayden slowly moved forward. She seemed so delicate, so fragile at this moment. He could feel her mind searching for something tangible to hold on to. His heart raced the closer he got to her. Her delicate scent enveloped him. His eyes stayed locked with her big, beautiful, warm eyes.

Emily reached out her hand to touch him. Her hand trembled as she felt the hard yet softness of his well-sculpted chest. "Did I die?" She had to reason she was dead. No man this beautiful would look at someone as common as her with such fire in his gaze. These strange events…she must be dead. Those men must have killed her.

"You are not dead Emily." Ayden cupped her cheek in his hand. Every thought he had of keeping his distance from her faded at this moment.

"You can't be real." She pushed at his chest and walked away from him. "Who are all you people?"

"Emily." Ayden walked over to her.

"Stay away from me!" she screamed.

Ayden immediately stopped. A flood of female voices rushed through his mind. *"No one but me will have you... I see the way they look at you...I will kill her for touching you...I love you more than life, Ayden..."*

"Ahhh!!" Ayden cried out. He would not do to Emily what he had done to every other woman who had loved him. She wanted him to stay away from her then he would. He was thankful she resisted him for it gave him the strength to keep his distance from her.

Emily watched Ayden walk away. She could feel his anguish though she didn't understand it. It tore at her as if it was her pain. "Someone please tell me what's going on," she quietly said.

Miranda walked over to Emily. She looked up and watched Ayden disappear into the woods.

"I will stand guard over Ayden," Michael offered up. He knew Miranda would be able to explain to Emily what was going on, so he would leave her to it. Ayden for whatever reason wasn't going to do it and someone had to. It was cruel to leave this woman wondering. This was unlike Ayden. Michael assumed Ayden must have his reasons, and then he left to stand guard over him.

"Please sit down." Miranda motioned over to a big tree. Emily did as she asked. The rest of the group kept their distance to give the women some privacy.

"What I am about to tell you will be hard to believe, but every word I say is true. Are you open minded enough to listen?"

Emily looked at Miranda's kind face. "Yes."

"Let me start from the beginning. Do you believe in Heaven and Hell?"

"Sort of."

"Heaven and Hell are very real, so to is Purgatory. Though each may not be what you originally believe them to be."

"I don't understand."

"Heaven is ruled by a being called Prolo and Hell is ruled by Lasax. Purgatory is ruled by Necoblas. These three are all ruled by the Creator." Miranda glanced over to Emily making sure she understood this so far. "When a soul dies it goes to Purgatory, from where Lasax and Prolo may choose souls to inhabit their realms. The Creator decides if a soul will go to either of them or if this soul will be reborn. When the Creator deems a soul worthy enough, this soul becomes immortal and is granted his or her paradise. Understand so far?"

"Yes, but I don't see what this all has to do with what is going on."

"You will." Miranda gently grabbed Emily's hand when she saw her trembling. "I know this is scary, believe me when Michael told me all of this it scared the hell out of me."

Emily latched onto Miranda's hand and prepared herself for what else Miranda was going to tell her.

"Ayden is the son of Asurul and Isa. Asurul was once a demon General and Isa was a guardian angel. These two fell in love with each other and this love changed Asurul. He risked everything to save Isa, as she did for him. The Creator would grant Asurul redemption provided he and Isa could pass a test. The price of failure was that both of them would become lesser-demons. Not wanting to chance Isa's soul, Asurul refused this test. Isa however knew her love for Asurul could pass any test. The Creator saw Asurul's refusal to take this test was doubt on Asurul's part of his love for Isa. Asurul tried to explain that he only wanted to protect Isa. The Creator turned Isa and Asurul mortal and forbade Lasax and Prolo from harming them.

Isa and Asurul passed the test. Their love grew stronger with each passing year, but since Asurul refused the test at first, the Creator cursed Ayden."

"Cursed?"

"Ayden had to find his soul mate. He would love and lose that love over and over until he found a woman that loved him, not only for his beauty but for who he was. This would prove the woman was indeed truly his soul mate. When he failed, Isa had the power to put him to sleep so that he may heal his wounded heart, however, when he slept this made him more vulnerable to Lasax's attacks."

"Attacks? Why would Lasax attack him?"

"No demon General had ever earned redemption before. He saw Asurul doing this as an insult to him and he swore since he couldn't harm Asurul he would kill Ayden. But the Creator granted Asurul warriors that would protect Ayden while he slept. These warriors became known as Asurul's demon hunters."

"Whoa wait, that man....your husband is he..."

"Yes, he was one of Asurul's hunters."

"Was?"

"Isa wanted the hunters to have the ability to earn redemption for their souls as well. A hunter is basically immortal. The only way he can be free is if Ayden finds his soul mate or they find theirs. I am Michael's soul mate. We are taking the same test Isa and Asurul did. In order to protect me, Michael was permitted to keep his demon skills. Gabriele and Ryker are also taking this test."

"Ryker is a hunter too?"

"No, Gabriele is."

"Ryo is another hunter and he and Jasmine are also taking this test."

"So all of Ayden's guardians have found their soul mates."

"Except for Saban."

"Ayden not only has to suffer the pain of love lost, he must also witness his hunters finding true love. Watch the joy and love that is denied him. " Emily stood up. She became very angry all of a sudden. "That sounds cruel."

Miranda slowly stood up. She never thought of it that way. It did seem cruel. "Ayden has a big heart and I doubt he resents his hunters finding happiness."

"I am sure he doesn't. But watching all this love must remind him of what he doesn't have."

"Why are you getting so angry?"

"I...I...don't know." Emily started to cry. Her heart ached for Ayden. She believed every word Miranda told her, she didn't know why, but she did. How many years, decades, or centuries did Ayden suffer?

"Hey, it's okay." Miranda hugged Emily and let her cry.

"Emily, don't cry," Ayden said as he walked up behind her. He heard every word they said. Emily's empathy for him touched him. Her tears for him tore at him.

Miranda let Emily go and walked away. Emily had to be the woman Ayden has been searching for, she just had to be.

"Let's leave them alone," Michael said, grabbing Miranda's hand gently.

"I didn't think our happiness might be hurting Ayden." Miranda wrapped her arms around Michael's neck and allowed him to pick her up.

"Come Miranda." Michael carried her into the woods.

"Don't cry for me," Ayden said, wiping the tears from Emily's face.

"It's all true isn't it?" Emily wrapped her arms around him and buried her face in his chest.

"Yes, it is." Ayden closed his eyes and held her tightly. He enjoyed the warmth of her embrace.

"Why was I able to hear you in my mind? See you in my dreams?" She held him closer.

"My soul called to yours and you embraced it." He nuzzled his cheek at the top of her head.

"I don't understand all of this. Who were those men? Were they demons?"

"Yes, they were demons. Emily, you must stay with us. Your life is in danger and only we can protect you."

"Why would my life be in danger? I am just an ordinary, recently divorced, slightly overweight woman. Why would the leader of Hell care if I live or die?"

"Because…" He held her tighter. It was his fault she was in danger, his fault Lasax would stop at nothing to destroy her. "My soul reached for yours."

Emily could hear the pain in his voice. She didn't know what to say, or even what to do. This was too much. But holding this man, who was once only a dream, felt right, felt safe, felt real.

Chapter 6

Tryton was a patience demon. Getting the hunters away from their mortal lovers would be a difficult task. He could already feel Prolo's Archangels coming. This didn't concern him. His main task was to kill those mortals. Ayden's Emily would have to wait until last; she would be the most guarded.

"Well mighty grand General, have you come up with a plan?" Evity ran her hands down his back. Evity so loved a man with power and right now Tryton had plenty of it. Only her master Lasax wielded more of Hell's power at this moment.

Alma growled as she sat there and watched Evity touch Tryton.

"Patience Evity." He turned around quickly and grabbed a hold of her. "Your beauty is remarkable." He let his eyes wander down her body.

"So is yours Tryton." She gave him a sexy smile.

Tryton growled at her then lunged. Evity didn't resist him. He tore at her clothes like an animal and she enjoyed his fire. Just with a mere thought his clothes were gone from his body. He pinned her against the wall, and with one forceful thrust, he entered her. He growled and bit her hard on the shoulder as he rode her. Tryton's cock stretched and filled her, making her moan. She raked her hands across his back and he delighted in the pain it brought him. He grunted and growled as he rode her faster and faster until his orgasm exploded. He felt her body quiver and knew she shared in his pleasure.

Alma became aroused watching Tryton take Evity like some animal in heat. He had to know she was still in here and no doubt this display was meant to torture her. Strangely Alma found this very arousing. She reached down and slowly stroked her clit through the fabric of her pants.

"That was a nice distraction," he said, licking Evity's lips.

"Mmmm," Evity purred.

Both of them sat down on the large bed. Tryton had already disposed of the occupants of this apartment. He glanced over at Alma and smiled at her. He saw the desire, the need in her eyes and he enjoyed it immensely. Let her suffer he thought. He reached out his hand and played with a strand of Evity's hair as he still held his gaze with Alma.

"Now, my beauty, we must concentrate on the task Lasax sent us to do." He brushed his fingers over her erect nipple.

"Command me and I will obey."

Tryton licked his lips then lowered her head down. "Suck my cock."

Evity moaned and took his cock into her mouth.

"Alma." Tryton motioned for her to come to him. Oh her eagerness was so good. "I want to watch you eat Evity's pussy." He ran his fingers over her lips and she tried disparately to take them into her mouth. "Do this for me?"

"Anything Tryton." Alma positioned herself between Evity's legs. Tryton lay down on the bed and kept his hand tangled in Evity's hair as she sucked his cock. He looked over to Alma as she began licking Evity's pussy. His eyes watched every stroke of her tongue. He felt Evity's moans vibrate on his cock.

"Yessss...."he purred. He grabbed a handful of Evity's hair and bobbed her head on his cock faster and faster, all the while he let his eyes feast on Alma's tongue in Evity's pussy. "Faster, lick faster," he growled.

Alma licked faster, wanting to please Tryton. The pleasure in his voice made her body come alive. She looked up at him as he moaned loudly. His eyes were closed tightly, his head tilted back as he licked his lips. That look of pleasure on his face made Alma's clit tighten. She watched his eyes slowly open, her eyes locked with his and it made her groan with desire.

Tryton sat up and laid Evity back onto the bed. He licked at her lips as he moved his hand down to Alma's head. He pushed down causing more of Alma's face to be buried into Evity's pussy. "Cum, my beautiful demon," Tryton purred against Evity's lips. He kissed her as her orgasm washed over her. He released Alma's head and pulled her up to them. He sat up and licked Evity's sweet juice from Alma's face.

"Please Tryton, fuck me," Alma begged.

Tryton climbed out of bed and got dressed. "Go Evity, scout out and gather some of the ancient Generals."

"As you wish Tryton." Evity got dressed then left.

"Tryton please."

He moved over to the bed. "Your body aches for mine doesn't it?" He ran his fingers lightly through her hair.

"You know it does." Alma reached up and began fiddling with the zipper to his pants.

Tryton smacked her hand away and moved from the bed. "You have to earn my cock, woman."

"You bastard," she growled. His laughter as he left the room only deepened her rage. She would find some mortal male to vent her anger. She could never hurt Tryton, no matter how awful he treated her.

ஐஐஐ

Tasmos glided across the sky. He was heading straight for a demon General. There were so many of them running around there was no way he could stop them all. The demons' need for sexual pleasure and the torment of others would distract them. Tasmos concluded that is why Lasax sent so many of them. But what was their target. Surely all of them couldn't be just for Ayden.

Screams of children caught Tasmos' attention. The demon he was in pursuit of would have to wait. He quickly followed the sounds of the children. Their fear raked over Tasmos, which caused his anger to surge. Just as he suspected, a group of lesser-demons were by the children. These poor children couldn't be anymore than five or six years old. The adult that was with them laid dead on the ground and the lesser-demons were feasting on him. There was nowhere for the small children to run and their fear gave the lesser-demons strength.

"Ssss, Archangel, sss," one cried out. The others immediately went on guard.

Tasmos landed in front of the children. He looked back at the huddled children. "Close your eyes," he said in a soothing voice. The children listened then he turned his attention back to the lesser-demons.

"What do you sssss, plan to do angel, ssss…"

Tasmos' spear appeared in his hands. The lesser-demons growled and started to wiggle and squirm toward him. Tasmos created a blast of energy to push back the beasts. With lightning fast speed he attacked, killing one beast after the other. When all of the lesser-demons lay dead, Tasmos turned his attention back toward the children.

"You can open your eyes now." He blocked the gruesome image from the children's minds.

Three women landed next to Tasmos. "You called us Tasmos?" they said in unison.

"Take these children somewhere safe." He was pleased the guardian angels responded to his call so quickly. They would ease the children's fears and ensure their safety.

Tasmos took back to the sky in pursuit of his original target. Lasax's disregard for mortal life angered Tasmos. He had to know his demons would kill many mortals. What was so important? Even Tasmos' Master, Prolo, seem to have urgency about him. Prolo cared more for mortals than Lasax did, but Tasmos knew that wasn't the cause of Prolo's anxiety.

Tasmos swooped down and grabbed a female demon. She was just about to kill an unlucky mortal male. "Tell me why you are here." Tasmos held her tightly as he soared higher in the sky.

"I am not telling you anything, angel," she hissed.

Tasmos let her go then swoop down and grabbed her again. He jetted back up into the sky. "Tell me or this time you will go splat."

"How do I know you won't kill me anyways?" She dug her nails into the flesh of his arm.

"I will give you a fighting chance if you tell me what I want to know. Otherwise I will drop you. The fall might not kill you, but it will sure hurt, then I will start slicing off pieces of you, saving your head for last." Tasmos started to loosen his grip on her.

"All right, Lasax has ordered us to kill all the mortal lovers of Asurul's demon hunters."

"What about Ayden?"

"We will be saving him for last."

"Why now, you had centuries to kill Ayden and his hunters."

"He has found his soul mate, besides, Master doesn't want him to be his equal."

"What does that mean?"

"I don't know angel. I told you all I know. Now take me back down to the ground."

Tasmos flew down and landed, letting the demon go. His spear appeared in his hand. He could see her eyes lock on to his silver dagger. Only silver forged by Prolo could kill an Archangel. All Archangels were ordered by Prolo to carry their silver dagger with them at all times. Tasmos couldn't figure out why his Master made such a law. Why have the one thing that could destroy him, so close to him all the time.

"You can try to reach my dagger demon, but you will never get that close to me."

"We will see, foolish angel," she hissed. She darted at him with incredible speed, but Tasmos was an ancient Archangel. He had fought many demons before and clearly this one was a fledgling. Tasmos used his spear to cut her head off. He guarded himself against the blast created by her soul being destroyed.

"Ayden will be Lasax's equal." Tasmos mulled this over in his mind. Why would Lasax care about Asurul's hunters? If Ayden was the target, why waste energy trying to destroy the hunters?

Tasmos took back to the sky. He had to meet up with two of his Sergeants. He didn't have time to worry about Asurul's hunters. Though in his mind he still owed the huntress Gabriele a debt, she destroyed Kannon for him, avenging his beloved Alisha. A debt he could never repay her for. He couldn't think about this. However the demon's words bothered him. The mortal lovers of the hunters were their target.

Chapter 7

Ayden cradled Emily in his arms while she slept. Ayden had sung the song of slumber to give her a few moments of peace. Her mind was overburden with all the strange things she just learned. Just holding her felt so good to him and he relished every moment. He didn't dare to think what it must be like to make love to her. Though he has touched her several times in her dreams, he wasn't prepared to hold her in real life. His fingers lightly traced over her face. Her skin was so soft. Her hair smelt of fresh flowers. He buried his nose in the wealth of her hair as he inhaled her fragrance. Her body fit against his perfectly, her small frame against his larger one. He couldn't take his eyes away from her. He ran his fingers lightly over her full lips.

"You are so beautiful to me, Emily," he whispered. But still the nagging presence of the demons stop him from totally losing himself in the moment. He couldn't rest now. He had to get her to safety.

"I hate to disturb you," Ryo said. Ayden looked so peaceful lying there in the grass with Emily.

"I feel the demons' presence, Ryo. Give me a few more moments."

"Okay." Ryo headed back over to the others.

"Well?" Gabriele asked.

"He wants a few more moments. And we are going to make sure he has it." Ryo gently grabbed Jasmine's hand and squeezed. He knew what Ayden felt. He had only found his soul mate just recently. He treasured every moment they had together. Jasmine squeezed his hand back and leaned her body next to his.

"There are too many demons roaming around," Michael spoke up.

"Yeah, we have to do something. With all of us together, won't they be able to hone in on Ayden faster?" Saban asked.

"Probably," Ryo answered.

Gabriele seemed agitated. "Damn it, I won't risk Ryker like this."

"Gabriele, we all feel the same way about our soul mates. But we must wait for Ayden to adjust," Ryo added.

"You know us puny mortals are not helpless," Ryker said. He pulled his arm away from Gabriele. "I am not made of glass."

"I didn't say you were helpless."

"Ryker has a point, Ryo." Jasmine looked up into his eyes. "If you hunters are always worried about us, you are going to get yourselves killed."

"Now is not the time for this," Saban injected.

Ayden stood up and helped Emily to her feet. He wanted to hold her for just a little while longer, but his hunters were becoming too agitated. He couldn't blame them, they had much to lose.

"What happened?" Emily asked as her eyes adjusted.

"You fell asleep."

"Then…" Emily looked around at the others. She wasn't dreaming. Everything started to spin. Everything swirled in her mind, demons, angels, Heaven, Hell….Ayden.

"It's okay." Ayden quickly wrapped his arm around her.

"What's going to happen now?" Emily sought the shelter of his arms. Strangely she felt safe there.

"We have to get you somewhere safe." He held her tighter. "Then I have to start destroying these demons before innocent people get hurt."

"They are going to hurt other people?" Emily left the warmth of his embrace. "We have to stop them."

"I have to stop them. You will be taken to a safe place."

"Then let's go." She couldn't let innocent people get hurt. She would deal with her own feelings later.

Ayden smiled down at her. He could see her concern in her eyes. He couldn't stop himself from picking her up. He took off and soared into the sky. "Kiss me," he whispered.

Emily looked deeply into his golden eyes. "Don't let go of me," her voice shook.

"Kiss me."

Emily raised her lips up to his. The moment their lips touched it felt like fire racing through her blood. Her body melted into his as he deepened their kiss. She couldn't breathe, or think. She held onto him tightly as they soared higher into the sky.

"Ayden," she sighed. She had never been kissed like that before. She could almost feel his soul in that kiss. Her body felt warm and alive. She could feel the wind blowing. She looked down and could see the clouds and yet she wasn't afraid. She knew he wouldn't let her fall. So she enjoyed the feeling of flight and feeling of his hard body next to hers.

"I must take you somewhere safe." Ayden looked deeply into her warm eyes.

"Okay, but hurry and help those people."

His smile warmed her heart. How could this beautiful man make her feel so alive, so scared, and somehow so loved all at once? Why does it feel like she had known him forever, yet they just met? Why did she feel like she belonged here in his arms? She searched for the answer in his golden eyes. If the eyes really were the window to someone's soul, then Ayden's soul was full of warmth, love and life.

"Ayden," she sighed as she laid her head against his chest. She felt his arm wrap around her tighter, so protectively it almost made her cry. She never felt so cherished before. Her stomach tingled as he soared higher and faster. This had to be a dream, a sweet wonderful dream. But feeling his hard body next to hers she knew all of this was real, no matter how crazy or far-fetched it was, it all was very real. Part of her was excited, the other part was terrified.

కుకుకు

"Let's go," Saban said, the second he got Ayden's message. The quadrants to where he and Emily were going popped into all the hunters' minds. He grabbed Ryker and threw him over his shoulder. He knew Gabriele would follow so he just took off. Saban felt strange, like something bad was going to happen. It was rare he felt like this, in fact the only other time he felt like this is when he died in his mortal life.

Saban heard Ryker groan as he leapt into the air to clear the small stream. His thoughts kept going back to his mortal life. He sacrificed so much to insure the safety of his people. Did he save them? He needed to know the answer. Somehow he knew Ayden could give him the answers he sought. His sweet beloved Geneva, a day never went by without him thinking about her.

He saw Ayden in the middle of the clearing. What was it about wooded areas that Ayden liked so much? Saban wasn't one to question. He sat Ryker down then scanned the area for Emily. She was sitting down by a pine tree and seemed to be lost in thought. Saban swore to himself that he would let nothing happen to Emily, especially after he seen Ayden and her together. They were meant to be. Ayden, something about this man invoked loyalty. Saban knew in his heart Ayden was meant to be something great. In his mortal life he followed a leader who was a great man. He died protecting this man. He couldn't help but wonder if his sacrifice meant anything.

"I wish you would stop carrying me like a sack of potatoes," Ryker grumbled.

"How else are you to keep up?" Saban smiled at Ryker and then walked over to Emily.

"What's your name?" Emily smiled up at him.

"Saban." He liked Emily's smile it reminded him of Geneva. In fact Emily appeared to be a lot like her.

"No last name?"

"I can't remember it." Saban scanned the area. They were safe for now.

"Emily you should sleep," Ayden said.

"I can't sleep." Emily was surprised when Saban removed his jacket and handed it to her. "Thank you."

"Your welcome." Saban continued his scan. He needed to talk to Ayden, but now wasn't the time. Ever sense Asurul took his soul from Purgatory, he had so many questions. He cleared his thoughts and thought about what he was suppose to be doing, protecting Ayden.

"I can put you to sleep for awhile if you would like. You look so tired." Ayden removed his shirt and made a pillow for her. He gently laid her down and began to sing.

Emily loved his voice. She couldn't understand the words he was singing, or even if they were words. The melody of his voice lulled her to sleep.

Ayden covered her up with Saban's jacket then kissed her lightly on the cheek. He looked up at Saban who was still scanning the area. He could tell Saban wanted to talk to him.

"Saban and I are going to do a perimeter check. Michael please stay with Emily." Ayden and Saban walked off into the woods.

"What is it you wish to ask?"

Saban abruptly stopped. "Now is not the time for this, Ayden."

"Why not, there is no threat at this moment. Now tell me what is bothering you."

Saban didn't know where to start. He bent down and scooped up a stick and began picking at the bark. "Do you know about my mortal life?"

"Yes, my father tells me about my hunters. You were a noble guard for a king. You had a wife, but no children. What was your wife's name?"

"Geneva." Saban smiled at just saying her name.

"You loved her very much didn't you?"

"Yes, she was everything." Saban still picked at the stick. Thoughts of Geneva comforted him. When he woken up and Asurul told him his fate all he could think of was Geneva. "Will I ever see her again?"

"I believe so."

Saban looked up at Ayden. "When, where?"

"Give me your hand."

Saban slowly extended his hand to Ayden. "Now think of her."

Ayden closed his eyes and images of Saban and a dark-haired woman flashed through his mind. "She was very beautiful," Ayden commented as he tried to focus harder.

"She was beauty," Saban added.

Ayden saw grayness. He grabbed Saban's hand tighter. A fog enveloped the grayness and it moved towards something. Countless souls were here, there were too many of them for Ayden to find Geneva. When Ayden saw Necoblas' ghastly figure he knew Geneva's soul was still in Purgatory.

"I can't seem to find her," Ayden lied. Saban didn't need to know that Geneva was still in Purgatory.

"Thank you for trying. Umm…" Saban paused.

"Continue."

"My king, did he survive? Was he worth my sacrifice?"

"Your king was truly a noble man. Your sacrifice saved his life and in turn saved thousands from being slaughtered."

Saban slid down the tree until he was in a squatting position. "What of Geneva? What happen to her?"

Ayden squatted next to Saban. "Do you really want to know?"

Saban looked into Ayden's golden eyes. "Yes…" He had to know.

"When she heard you had died, her heart broke and she died a couple weeks later."

"How?"

"In her sleep, her soul wanted so much to be with yours, it went looking for you."

Saban choked back the tears. He had hoped that she moved on and found someone to make her happy. She deserved as much. But to know that her love for him was so great that she followed him in death…. "Will I ever see her again?"

"Her soul will find yours."

"How do you know?" Hoping against hope that Ayden wasn't just saying what he wanted to hear.

Ayden sat down and looked out over the forest. "I can't explain it. I just know this."

Saban saw the distress look in Ayden's face and knew his words were true. This man did know these things, not even he knew the extent of his gifts. Ayden was truly a great man. Saban's resolve to protect him strengthen ten fold.

"I feel your pain, my hunter." Ayden slowly stood up. "Know that Geneva is waiting for you and someday you will be together again, let it bring you comfort." Ayden walked away to give Saban a few moments alone.

The tears rolled down Saban's face, tears of joy and sorrow. "Geneva," he whispered.

Chapter 8

Emily slowly woke up. Her body was a bit sore from sleeping on the ground. She sat up and looked around. Ayden was talking with his hunters. Miranda, Ryker and Jasmine were readying the camp.

"Are you feeling better?" Saban asked.

"Yes, I think."

"You are safe with any of us. We wouldn't let anything happen to you." He smiled at her then walked over to Ayden.

She saw that all the non-hunters were busy setting up camp. She had no idea what Ayden was saying to his hunters, but she assumed it had to do with the demons he mentioned earlier.

"Well I can't just sit here and do nothing," she said to herself. She got up and brushed off her pants. She felt uncomfortable just sitting around. She had to do something to help, though what, she had no idea. Her thoughts were so jumbled up. It was like she was plopped down into some strange supernatural movie. Clearly her part was the damsel in distress. She walked over to Miranda. "Is there something I can do to help?"

"Sure, take all the medical supplies over to the tent Ryker is putting up."

Emily gathered up the first-aid boxes and headed over towards Ryker. She waited for him to finish putting the tent up. "You look like you have done this many times before," she commented.

"I have." Ryker finished up then turned to her. "Those need to go in here?"

"Yeah." She handed him the boxes.

"You are looking a little better," he said as he placed the boxes into the tent along with the food supplies. Ayden had instructed them to set up camp here, so that was what he was going to do. He let the women help so they would feel useful. He understood their need for this. Hell, he wished he could help Gabriele more.

"I am still trying to sort all of this out."

Ryker smiled at her. "You will. It took me awhile to adjust to this crazy stuff."

"Ryker be on guard, I feel the presence of several demons coming this way." Gabriele's voice filled his mind.

Emily jumped back a little when Ryker quickly pulled his pistol out and then grabbed her and placed her behind him.

"What's wrong?" Emily asked as her eyes scanned everywhere.

"Take it easy soldier boy; you are going to scare Emily."

"Sorry." Ryker disarmed his gun then placed it back into its holster. "Gabriele went on alert, so I immediately did the same. I am a bit more jumpy than she is, I'm afraid."

"How did you know she was?" Emily looked over to Gabriele. She still had her shotgun in her hand.

"I can just sense it, besides, she told me to be on guard." Ryker gently grabbed Emily's arm and escorted her back towards Miranda. "It's hard to explain. But sometimes I can hear Gabriele's voice in my head, especially when we are in danger."

"You can?" Emily remembered the countless times she heard Ayden's voice in her head.

"I can hear Michael's," Miranda added. "And I am sure Jasmine hears Ryo's . It's something to do with being soul mates. That's what I think anyways."

"Soul mate," Emily whispered, looking over at Ayden. She was trying so hard to be strong, but all of this was almost too much to comprehend. She took a deep breath and tried to steady her emotions. Now wasn't the time to fall to pieces. These people had something important to do and the last thing they needed was to babysit some hysterical woman. She was never the one to just sit around and act all helpless. She closed her eyes and tried to center herself using the yoga techniques Shelly taught her.

"Shelly and Diane." Emily's heart started pounding in her chest. She looked over toward Ayden and saw he was heading towards her with a concern look in his eyes.

"I sense your fear. What's wrong?" Ayden pulled her towards him and held her tightly.

"My friends, Shelly and Diane are they going to be okay?"

"Picture them in your mind for me." Ayden closed his eyes and focused, the image of two women popped into his head. "Michael."

"Yes." Michael hurried over towards him.

"I want you to guard Emily while I…"

"No, I am going with you." Emily broke free of his embrace. "What is happening?" She saw the strange look on Ayden's face. "What happened to them?"

"I am not sure."

"Something is wrong, isn't it?"

"I don't know."

"Then let's go and make sure they are okay."

"I won't risk you."

"You don't have a choice. Either you take me with you or I will go by myself."

"Emily…"

"I mean it." Emily crossed her arms and glared up at Ayden. She wasn't backing down. Shelly and Diane might be in trouble. They won't know who Ayden is and what would be worse, if they treated him like some sort of freak or something.

"You don't want me being alone with them do you?" Ayden's heart sank. This is how it started with the other women who loved him. Their vile jealousy destroyed them in the end, Emily couldn't be jealous… not Emily, not this fast.

"What in the hell are you talking about? Why would I care if you were alone with them? I just don't want you to freak them out."

Ayden stroked Emily's hair gently. "I am sorry." The fear she had for her friends started to fill him. His heart pounded as rapidly as hers did.

"Ummm…do you want me to get her friends?" Michael asked.

"No, stay here." Ayden picked up Emily. "We will be back tomorrow morning." With that he took flight with Emily cradled in his arms.

"What was that about?" Miranda said, grabbing Michael's hand.

"She was worried about her friends and she wasn't letting him leave without taking her with him." Michael started to chuckle.

"What is so funny?"

"Her determination reminds me of you." He caressed her face.

"Oh, Michael what if those demons have already killed her friends." Miranda fought back the memories of finding her best friend Amy's mutilated body.

"Miranda please stop torturing yourself over Amy's death. You couldn't have stopped it."

"I know, but it's a memory I would rather not have."

"Where is Ayden going?" Ryo asked.

"To take Emily's friends somewhere safe." Michael held Miranda close and gently caressed her, trying to soothe the pain of her memories. Miranda was so strong, what other woman could literally survive Hell and still be sane.

Ryo looked at Miranda. She was sheltering herself in the safety of Michael's arms. He didn't want to disturb them but he could feel the demons closing in.

"I know Ryo," Michael nodded his head toward him. "give me a minute, then we will plan our attack."

"Alright." Ryo left the two and headed over to Jasmine.

"Is she all right?" Jasmine latched onto his arm.

"She will be." Ryo didn't like this. Ayden shouldn't have gone off by himself. And why were the demons still advancing? Surely they had to know Ayden wasn't here.

"What's wrong?" Jasmine asked, seeing the distress look in Ryo's eyes.

"Wait here a moment." Ryo went over where Ryker stored the weapons. He picked out a pistol and couple clips of ammo. He went back over to Jasmine. "Here, take this and keep it on you at all times."

"I have never shot a gun before." Jasmine felt the coldness of the steel barrel in her hand.

Ryo attached the pistol holster around her waist then put the clips of ammo into the slots. He gently caressed her hips and nuzzled his cheek against the top of her head. "Please carry this."

"I'll carry it, but I am not sure how effective I will be with it."

"Aim for the head." Ryo felt her arms go around him, pulling him closer to her.

"That bad huh?" she asked, holding him tighter.

"Yeah." Ryo ran his hand down her silky black hair. Few words were needed between them. They seemed to know what each other were thinking.

"Okay listen up people," Michael said. He handed Miranda one of his pistols. "Remember to brace yourself before you shoot that."

"I'll remember."

"For whatever reason a bunch of demons are still advancing towards us. I don't want them to make it to this camp. So I want Gabriele and Ryo to come with me. Saban, you will guide the rest away from here."

"Hold up, there is no way I am letting Gabriele go fight a bunch of demons without me," Ryker spoke up.

"Ryker, I know what I am doing." Gabriele knew Michael wanted those demons as far away from Miranda as possible. She couldn't blame him. She wanted Ryker away from here too. They were mortal and though Ryker was a skilled soldier he was no match for a demon General.

"No, damn it. I won't let her go."

"You have no choice," Michael's voice boomed. "I don't have the time to argue with you. Gabriele is a skilled huntress. You will have to curb your masculine instinct to protect her."

"I am sure Miranda and Jasmine don't want you two going out there as well."

"Miranda is not your concern." Michael headed over to Ryker.

"Michael, Ryker is right." Miranda grabbed his arm and stopped him. "I don't want you going out there and facing God knows how many demons."

"I have to do this. I won't be able to fight if they make it here. Please understand this Miranda."

"Ryker, I love the fact you want to protect me, but we have no time to argue. We know how to fight these demons. I really need you to help Saban protect Ryo and Michael's soul mates. I am not trying to patronize you in anyway. But your skills would be better suited to protect them."

"Gabriele…" Ryker pulled her to him and kissed her softly. "Then go demon huntress, but remember where you go I will follow."

"Ryker." Gabriele knew what he meant. If she died so would he.

Saban gathered the supplies they would need. He watched the couples saying goodbye to each other. His heart ached for Geneva, but at the same time he knew the other hunters had accepted him by intrusting him to protect their soul mates.

"When we have killed all the demons I will contact you Saban," Michael said.

Saban nodded his head then grabbed Jasmine and Miranda gently by the arm and guided them to the other side of the camp.

"Don't get hurt huntress," Ryker said, caressing her cheek.

"I won't, now go with Saban." Gabriele watched Ryker and the others walk into the forest. She couldn't fail; she had to kill every one of those demons before they had a chance to get to Ryker.

"Come on Gabriele it's time to hunt." Michael dashed off. Ryo and Gabriele were right behind him.

കാകാകാ

"It worked, very good Tryton," Evity clapped.

"Thank you, thank you." He did a mock bow. "Now while the hunters are chasing around those peons, I will send some of the best Generals to kill the mortals." Of course the best Generals had already been killed by those damn hunters throughout the years. But he would have to work with what he had. He knew he could count on Evity; her power rivaled that of Kali's. Oh how he wished he had Kali, Manus and Syn here, they were three of Hell's best Generals. Those damn hunters....Tryton seethed. However if they could defeat those three, he would be wise not to underestimate them. Something most of those other idiot demons would surely do.

"I will block their mental pathways, so they can't call out for the hunters to help them."

"Go, the sooner you do that the better this plan will work." Tryton watched Evity race off. "Only one hunter to protect those mortals, and the newest hunter at that." Tryton was pleased with himself. His plan was working perfectly. Ayden taking off like that just sped up everything, but why wait. Now to head for Ayden, he wanted to kill the son of Asurul himself.

"You go find those other demons and bring them here," he growled at Alma.

"Yes Tryton." She hurried off.

"Vengeance will be mine, Asurul. You were to make me your second in command before you became a traitor. Do you know how long I had to grovel to those other ancient Generals when you abandon me?" Tryton shouted up at the sky. Asurul would pay for what he did, for betraying him.

Syn loved to torment him simply because he was Asurul's protégé. But he needed to learn Syn's skill with a sword. Kali was only interested in him as a lover which suited him just fine. But Manus, his body still shivered at the thought of the vile acts Manus made him perform. He needed Manus' skill as a tracker. Anger raged in Tryton as he thought about everything he went through to rise up in the ranks of Hell. One thought however he wouldn't acknowledge, though it kept creeping up in his mind. He loved Asurul as a brother once, strange he thought that, but he did, which made Asurul's betrayal that much more painful to endure.

"Rrrrrr," he growled as he tried to stop that thought from entering his mind. He started to think of killing Ayden, Asurul's beloved son. These thoughts fueled his anger and made him focus back on his plan.

If only Lasax and Prolo hadn't trapped Asurul in his paradise, he could have killed Asurul as well. "Oh well I can't have everything." Tryton chuckled. "When I am Lasax's right hand, Asurul, then I will destroy your soul."

Chapter 9

"Tryton!!" Asurul growled. He had trained Tryton himself. "Damn it. I have to go to Ayden."

"Asurul stop this," Isa said, grabbing his arm. "You are going to really injure yourself."

Asurul was filled with small cuts as he tried to fight his way out. "No barrier will stop me."

Tryton was an eager student and learned quickly during his training. Asurul knew Tryton's skill and he feared for Ayden.

"You don't understand Isa."

"Then tell me so I can understand."

Asurul kept his eyes focused on the barrier. "I trained that Grand General…I can't tell you anymore."

"Tell me Asurul. You know I will not judge you."

Asurul was silent for a moment. "When I trained him he learned quickly. I soon discovered he had a bloodlust that surpassed my own." Asurul kept his eyes locked on the barrier. His words came out slow and emotionless. He couldn't stand for his beloved Isa to hear about when he was a demon, but he had to make her understand why he had to break free and go to Ayden. "Tryton took delight in torturing fledglings and lesser-demons, though I think Syn influenced this particular behavior. Tryton would watch all of us ancient Generals, soaking up everything he saw. When he was allowed to accompany me to Earth he…" Asurul paused. He felt Isa's hand on his back as she gently caressed him. She was always so accepting of him. He wanted to tell her everything, his mortal life, his time as a demon General, but he couldn't. So telling her this small part of what he was tore him apart.

"Asurul," Isa quietly said.

He moved away from her. "When Tryton came to Earth with me, he tortured and tempted several mortal souls, more so, than even Syn would have done. The delight he took in corrupting and destroying these souls was beyond anything I could ever do."

"Asurul, of course it would be beyond what you could do."

"You don't understand, because you only wish to see the good in me. For me to say he surpassed me…this made him truly a monster. Now our son is out there with this monster hunting him down. I can't just sit here and do nothing."

Asurul yelled and charged at the barrier again. His skin got cut with each blow he delivered.

"Stop this!!" Isa cried. She couldn't bear to see Asurul destroy himself like this. That barrier would more than likely slice him to ribbons.

Asurul turned towards Isa. Her tear stained face tore at his heart. "Isa…" He cupped her face in his bloody hands. "I have to get out of here. Our son needs me."

"The Creator has forbidden us to interfere. Prolo and Lasax were allowed to place this barrier up. You can't go against the Creator. Don't you think I want to help our son too?"

"I know you do." Asurul saw his blood on her face. He did this to them. He watched both of them suffer through the years because of him. He will not sit idly by and let it continue. Damn his soul, if that's the price he has to pay for protecting his family. Ayden has found his soul mate and now his purpose was clear. Asurul couldn't, he wouldn't sit by and watch Tryton destroy everything. If

Ayden dies, a part of Isa will die, hell a part of him will die too. There will be no paradise for her. Her beautiful soul has suffered so much because she chose to love him.

"ARRGGHHH!!!" Asurul screamed and charged at the barrier again.

Isa could only stand there and watch Asurul destroy himself. She sank to the floor and wept.

ೞೞೞ

"Shelly, Diane!" Emily called out as she entered their small house. It was too quiet. Emily couldn't stop the feeling of dread that washed over her.

"Let me go in first." Ayden gently pushed her aside. He scanned the area. Demons had already been here. He couldn't sense any signs of life at all in the house.

"Shelly, Diane!!" Emily cried out again.

"They are not here," Ayden said quietly. He slowly made his way through the house. The backdoor was knocked completely off its hinges.

"Oh my God," Emily said when she saw the door. "Are they dead?"

"I don't believe so."

"But…" Emily braced herself for anything.

"Demons have taken them."

"Then they are dead."

"No…they're not." Ayden could feel the residue of the women's fear. The demons took them as bait. God knows what Emily's friends will be forced to endure while they were the demon's captives.

"Ayden, what will happen to them? Tell me the truth."

"I believe the demons are using them as bait to trap me. I am sorry Emily. If you never knew me…"

"Don't…" Emily placed her fingers on his lips to silence him. "Please don't think like that." Emily turned from him and looked over the kitchen. How many hours did she spend in this room? This room was full of so many good memories.

Ayden reached out and touched her shoulders. He closed his eyes and focused. Her memories danced in his mind. All the laughter, comfort and support Shelly and Diane had given her over the years filled him with warmth. "I will find them Emily."

"But you said it was a trap for you." Emily turned around and gazed into his eyes.

"They are important to you, which make their safety all important to me. I will be careful."

"I don't know…what if you get hurt. But we can't just sit here and do nothing. They are with demons for Christ sakes. What are they doing to them?" Emily started to cry.

"Please don't cry. I will get them back, but I will have to go alone. Shhh, don't cry." He wiped the tears from her face, as he did her tears evaporated and turned into sparkles of brilliant light. He had to take away her pain. He couldn't stand her tears.

Emily gasped and watched the beautiful sparkles of light fill the room. "Ayden…" She could feel his need to comfort her, to take away her tears and turn her sorrow into beauty. She looked into his eyes. The beauty of this one moment threatened to make her cry again.

"I will find them and take them to safety."

Emily reached up and caressed his face. "Thank you." She got up on her tiptoes and raised her lips to his. She gently kissed him. His heart soared; she had reached for him this time. He cupped the back of her head and deepened the kiss. This moment was theirs. All other thoughts temporarily left his mind. He kissed her with everything he had. He wanted her to feel his love for her. Every fear, every doubt he had melted away with this kiss. She was his salvation.

Ayden heard the voices of demons taunting him. His beautiful moment with Emily had to end. "I must go."

"No, we must go." Emily stroked his cheek.

"Emily, it will be too dangerous." Ayden kissed her softly all over her face.

"It will be too dangerous to leave me alone. At least you will know I am all right if I am with you."

Ayden knew she was right. "Promise me you will do what I say."

"I promise."

Ayden hugged her tightly. If only they had more time. "Let's go, a demon has given away where your friends are being held." Ayden looked at her. "What we might find may be disturbing are you sure you want to witness it?"

"Yes, Shelly and Diane would do this for me."

"Okay, let's get you a gun of some sort. You shoot the demons in the head and only if they find you. Understand?"

"Yes."

"Emily, you will witness me killing beings that look like humans. Just remember these beings, though once human, they are now demons."

"I will be all right, don't worry about me. You concentrate on keeping yourself safe and helping me get my friends back."

Ayden smiled. Her courage and strength was beyond compare. "Let's go." He scooped her up into his arms, once they left the house he took to the sky.

Her thoughts filled his mind as he glided across the sky. He could feel her fear for her friends. He sent waves of reassurance to her trying to ease her mind. He looked down into her face as her thoughts of him raced through his mind. She was trying to rationalize her feelings for him. And yet she took comfort in her feelings for him. He held her tighter as he picked up speed. He wished he could block her thoughts. She deserved some privacy. He couldn't stop from reading her thoughts. He knew how to shut his mind to her. But how did he block her thoughts from flooding him. He felt her snuggle up against him, trying to find some comfort.

"It will be all right Emily." He kissed the top of her head.

"Thank you Ayden."

He could feel her trust in him. Her thoughts were coming rapidly now and he had to focus to keep his mind focused on the demon's taunts. They were almost there. He would not let Emily's friends be murdered by those demons. She trusted him to make everything all right and that was exactly what he was going to do.

Chapter 10

"Leave me alone!" Shelly cried out as a male demon groped at her.

"How many times are you going to fuck those two?" Shala rolled her eyes. Her male companions had raped the two mortal women repeatedly since she and Luca brought them here. The blonde hair woman had passed out twenty minutes ago, which only left this mortal woman awake. If Shala had a heart she might feel pity for the two, especially this one who was being raped by two male demons now.

"Ayden will be here soon." Luca played with Diana's hair as she lay lifeless in her lap.

Shala looked back at Shelly when she heard gagging noises. "Would you two hurry up, we must prepare for Ayden." She watched as both men thrust their cocks harder into Shelly, one in her mouth the other in her pussy.

"I want to see if she can swallow my cock," one of the males groaned.

"Don't you dare kill that mortal, we need her to trap Ayden."

Luca got up and walked over to Shala. She watched the males ravage Shelly. "Oh, come on let him kill her."

"No damn it." Shala pushed Luca away from her. This was her big chance to impress Lasax and she would kill all three of these pathetic demons to do it. However, she needed these three idiots to help her kill Ayden.

Luca strolled over to the male who was thrusting his cock violently into Shelly's pussy. "Mmm, when we have killed Ayden I want you to fuck me like that."

"With pleasure," he growled. He pulled his cock out and stood up stroking his cock until his juice sprayed into the other male's mouth.

"Yummy," the other purred, licking his lips as he thrust his cock faster and harder into Shelly's mouth.

"Hurry up!" Shala was growing impatient with the two males.

He thrust two more times and held his cock down Shelly's throat as he came. "Drink all of it mortal." He grinded his hips against her then finally pulled his cock from her mouth. Shelly coughed and spat then rolled over to her side.

"Leave the mortals where they are." Shala took out her daggers.

"How do we kill Ayden?" Luca asked.

"Painfully," Shala said, licking her lips. She told the others where to go and instructed one of the males to stay with the mortal women.

Shelly rolled over and saw Diane just laying there. Shelly's body was bruised and beaten, but still she managed to crawl over to Diane. "Hey, are you all right?" she asked, stroking Diane's hair. She looked up at the dark-haired man who was standing guard over them. He was too busy looking out the window to notice anything else at this moment.

"What is happening?" Diane's voice was a mere whisper.

"I don't know..." Shelly lay next to Diane and wrapped her arm around her.

ଚ୨ଚ୨ଚ୨

"Stay here. I will know if you are in trouble." Ayden ran his fingers through her soft brown hair. He could feel the presence of four demons, two males and two females. He couldn't bear to leave Emily here alone, but he had no choice. He had to keep her out of sight. He knew the demons would be too focused on killing him to bother scanning for her.

"Are Diane and Shelly alive?"

"Yes, now stay here."

"Be careful." Emily pulled him down to her and kissed him.

"I will be." He brushed his fingers lightly over her lips and gazed into her beautiful face for a moment.

The next thing she knew he was gone, as if he just disappeared right in front of her eyes. She held onto the pistol tightly as she leaned up against the tree. She was so afraid for Diane and Shelly, but more so for Ayden. This was a trap for him and he was risking his life to save her friends. Two women he didn't even know, and yet he didn't hesitate to rescue them. "Please be okay," she prayed quietly.

Ayden landed softly on the roof. The demons' vile essence was everywhere. Slowly two hand blades appeared in his hands. Asurul taught him how to use these weapons well.

"Use your speed and strength. Strike fast, strike with deadly precision, then get away from your enemy, don't give him a chance to strike back." Asurul's words echoed in Ayden's mind

He spotted a dark-haired man climbing up the side of the house. He waited for the right moment to attack. The demon smiled at him then lunged for him. Judging by this demon's speed, he wasn't a fledgling. Ayden moved out of the way just before the demon attacked, he swung his arm and embedded one of his hand blades into the demon's back.

Before the demon could react, Ayden grabbed a handful of his hair and tilted his head back, with one powerful stroke of his hand blade he severed the demon's head. He braced himself for the blast of the demon's soul being destroyed. He launched himself in the air, avoiding the attack of the red-haired female.

"Get back here," Luca growled as she leapt up after him. She was shocked when he flew at her, grabbing her by the waist. "No demon can fly," she hissed, pounding on his arm.

"I am no demon." Ayden flew higher then threw her towards the ground. Luca hit the ground so hard she bounced. She laid on the ground rolling around in agony.

Ayden landed beside her and with one swipe, he cut her head off. The blast of her soul being destroyed knocked him back. He winced when he felt claws dig into his back.

"Die, son of Asurul," Shala yelled as she embedded her dagger into his back.

Ayden reached behind and grabbed her, flipping her over him. He blocked the pain of the dagger and raced at her. She leapt into the air, but he managed to catch her. Ayden heard the sound of women screaming. He quickly sliced off Shala's head and threw her body down, avoiding the blast.

He flew down and raced into the house. A male demon had a small petite Latino woman in his arms with a dagger to her throat.

"Drop your weapons Ayden," the demon hissed.

Ayden did as he asked. "Let the woman go."

"Why, she makes a good shield."

"Let her go."

"Or?" The demon licked Shelly's face. Diane started to scream, giving Ayden the brief distraction he needed. The second the demon looked over towards Diane, Ayden raced over and punched the demon in the face. He grabbed the arm that held the dagger and pried it away from Shelly. Once she was free he pushed her away from the demon. Ayden broke the demon's arm and turned the knife around and stabbed the demon in the chest. He held out his hand and his hand blade flew over into his hand.

"Don't look," Ayden said to the two women, and then he decapitated the demon. He raced over and used his body to protect the two women from the blast of the demon's soul being destroyed.

Ayden took off his shirt and handed it to Shelly. She helped Diane put it on. Ayden spotted a comforter on the sofa. He went over and grabbed it and handed it to Shelly. He looked at the two women. They were bloody and beaten, and the blonde-haired one looked to be in shock.

"Who are you?" Shelly said, wrapping her and Diane in the comforter.

"I am Ayden. Emily is with me."

"Oh my God, is she all right?" Shelly asked.

"Yes, she is just fine. Do you need medical attention? Is there anyone else here?" Ayden scanned the house but couldn't sense any human life, other than the two women.

"They killed the old couple that lived here," Shelly quietly answered.

"Where are their bodies?" Ayden wanted to give them a proper burial.

"They…they…" Shelly started to cry. "Those…oh my God… those monsters ate the bodies."

Ayden went over to her and wrapped his arm around her. "Shh, I will get Emily, stay here."

Shelly nodded her head and hugged Diane tighter.

"Ayden!!!"

"Emily!" Ayden raced out of the house. He heard the sound of gunfire. His heart beat heavy and fast in his chest. He didn't sense any other demons. He scanned the area as he hurried towards where he left her. He couldn't sense any demons at all. When he rounded the corner a tall, blonde-haired man was approaching Emily. She had shot him four times in the chest, but it didn't seem to faze him.

"Leave her alone," Ayden growled, lunging for the man. But before he could grab hold of the man, he took to the air. The man landed a few hundred feet in front of them. "Stay behind me, Emily."

"Why didn't he die?" Emily asked as she dropped the gun.

"He is an Archangel." Ayden's eyes scanned the man's body and spotted the silver dagger that was strapped to the man's thigh.

"An angel, but why was he trying to take me?"

"I don't know, just stay there."

"Son of Asurul, I am Erastus," he bellowed. A spear slowly appeared in his hand. "I will not sit idly by and watch the son of a demon become my Master's equal."

Erastus took to the air. He had no wish to hurt the mortal woman with Ayden; she was only used to bait him out.

"Run to the house, your friends need you, Emily."

"What about you?"

"Just go." Ayden took to the air after Erastus. He flew with speed he didn't know he possessed. He had to catch this Archangel. Anger boiled in him. This being dared to attack his Emily. Ayden had a sudden burst of speed, he grabbed Erastus by his ankles, forcing him to the ground.

His hand blades emerged, but he knew they were useless against an Archangel. He had to get the silver dagger from him. Erastus attack with great speed and skill,

Ayden blocked a few of the strikes with his blades but a couple managed to pierce him. He ignored the pain and focused on the dagger. He dodged the next strike and managed to get near Erastus.

"I am not so easily defeated," Erastus growled as he embedded his spear into Ayden's thigh.

Ayden grimaced but reached out for the dagger. Once it was in his hand he stabbed Erastus in the side. Erastus fell to the ground. His body shook and trembled, then he lay there motionless.

Ayden fell to the ground and grabbed his thigh. He had to stop the bleeding somehow. Ayden watched in amazement as his wound slowly began to close. Within moments it was like he was never injured. He ran his hand over where the wound use to be, not a mark was left.

Ayden sat there for a moment the words the Archangel said repeated over and over in his mind. "His Master's equal…" Ayden quietly said. He had no idea what Erastus was talking about. He ran his hand over the rip in his jeans where Erastus' spear had stabbed him. He knew he had the power to heal others, but the speed in which his body healed itself was unbelievable. "How can I do that?" Ayden mulled over the countless little things he had discovered about himself through the years. He could read anyone's mind by simply touching them, heal and comfort others….the list went on in his mind.

"Ayden are you all right?"

He felt Emily's hands on his shoulder.

"Yes."

Emily went around to the front of him and sat down. "Are you sure?" Her hands went to his thigh. "You are bleeding."

"Was bleeding." Ayden grabbed her hand and pulled her to him. "Are you injured?" He looked into her eyes, seeking comfort.

"No…" She cupped his face in her hands. "What's wrong?" He had such a lost look in his eyes, it made her heart ache.

"I…" Ayden ran his hands through her hair. "I don't understand why I am."

"What?"

"I can't expect you to understand. Hell, I don't know how to explain it."

"Try me." Emily moved over and sat down beside him.

"You will think I am crazy."

"After everything I have seen in these last few days, trust me, nothing will seem crazy to me." Emily reached over and grabbed his hand. He was hurting inside, she could feel it as if it was her pain.

"Ever since I can remember, my parents told me how I came to be. Their talk of angels and demons seem natural to me. Until I met this little girl when I was no more than nine years old, she somehow wandered onto our ranch. We talked for an afternoon before my mother found out about this girl and sent her away. That is when I realized I wasn't like everyone else; I would never be like everyone else. My father told me of the dangers of the demons, and that is why I was forbidden to play with other children." Ayden turned to Emily. "You see, a lesser-demon can take a form of a child if a General gives him or her the power." Ayden squeezed Emily's hand.

"That must have been lonely not to have other children to play with."

"It was, but my mother tried to make up for it."

"Are your parents…ummm…dead?"

"In the conventional sense, yes they are. In order to pass the test the Creator gave them, they had to become mortal again and live their mortal lives on Earth. This is the time I was born. They died when I was only twenty-one years old. My mother just went to sleep and never woke up. My father was so distraught he died of a broken heart four days after her. It always seemed to me that my father was made to suffer. The images of him weeping for my mother, will always been burnt in my mind." Ayden stood up and helped Emily to her feet. He grabbed her hand and started walking towards the house.

"Wait, I want to know more about you. I want to…help somehow." Emily pulled on his arm to make him stop.

"You have no idea how much you are helping me. We should get back to the house so I can send your friends to sleep, so they can have a few moments of peace." He didn't have the luxury of time. He wanted so much to tell Emily everything, so she would know who he was. But right now he didn't even know who he was anymore.

"Yeah, your right." Emily squeezed his hand tighter. She wished she understood what he was going through. Maybe then she might be able to soothe his worries.

"Emily." He stopped and turned to her. "You just being here with me and accepting me for who, or for that matter, what I am….soothes me beyond words to let you know how much."

"How did you know what I was thinking?"

Ayden raised her hand up to his lips and gave it a soft kiss. "When you touch me every thought you have fills my mind. I have tried to block the images to give you a measure of privacy, but I don't know how to." Ayden released her hand and started walking back up to the house. Emily hurried behind him and grabbed his hand and squeezed it tightly.

"Well, I will never be able to complain you don't listen to me, huh?" She chuckled. She deliberately thought of lots of silly scenarios, mostly involving monkeys and dancing dogs as she held his hand. His laughter warmed her heart and her acceptance of him warmed his.

They walked back to the house. Emily rushed over to Diane and Shelly.

"Emily you are okay?" Shelly latched on to her.

Emily hugged her tightly. She didn't want to know what those two had to endure at the hands of those demons, judging by their beaten bodies it was awful. Ayden went over to Diane and carried her to one of the rooms upstairs. She had passed out again. Emily helped Shelly up to her feet. Ayden came back down and lifted Shelly up and carried her to another upstairs bedroom so she could rest. Emily cleaned them up the best she could.

Ayden looked around the house and grounds making sure they were safe for now, then Emily and Ayden went up to check on Diane. Shelly was there with her.

"Hey it's okay, he is with me." Emily hurried to the bed and grabbed Diane's hand.

"He saved us," Shelly added as she grabbed Diane's other hand.

"I can erase what happened to you," Ayden said, sitting on the end of the bed

"You can do that?" Emily asked.

"Yes, but they will have no memory at all of the last two days."

Shelly looked to Diane. There was no way Diane was going to handle what they went through. It all seemed like a nightmare now. "But I will not understand what's happening." Shelly looked up at Emily. "How will I be able to help you?"

"Don't you worry about me."

Shelly thought it over. "Okay do it."

Emily moved out of the way as Ayden sat down next to Diane. He placed his hands in hers and concentrated. Every awful moment Diane lived through he was forced to endure along side her. Emily watched the pain cross over Ayden's face. After ten minutes he let go of Diane's hand and she fell asleep.

"Alright, now you," Ayden said, breathing hard.

He reached out his hands and Shelly gently grabbed them. As before he relived every moment of Shelly's torment all in ten minutes. Such a bombardment of memories drained him. He released her hands and fell to the floor.

"Ayden!" Emily hurried over to him. She helped him up to his feet and guided him down the hall to another bedroom and sat him down on the bed. "Why didn't you tell me that doing that would hurt you?"

"I will be fine in a moment. My small discomfort was worth your friends finding some peace."

Emily laid him down and climbed in the bed next to him. She snuggled up next to him, laying her head on his chest. "Are you safe here for a little while?" Emily asked.

"Yes, for a little while."

"You will never be truly safe will you?"

"No." He held her closer to him. "But I feel peace at this moment." He kissed the top of her head. He wanted so much to make love to her, but not here, not now. He was too weak and he must gather his strength back up quickly. He had to be ready to protect her. And this place where great evil stains everything was not the place he wanted to show his love for her.

"When I have rested a little, I will take your friends somewhere safe." Ayden wondered if there was a safe place to hide them with so many demons roaming around.

"You sleep, I will watch out for any demons." Emily said, wrapping her arm tighter around him in a protective manner.

Ayden smiled and nuzzled his chin on the top of her head.

Chapter 11

"Michael there is so many of them," Gabriele said as she blasted a female demon with her shotgun. All three of the hunters were surprised by the large number of demons that had gathered in one place. All of these Generals sent to attack them. But why so many?

"Regardless we fight." Michael charged at a male demon. He wouldn't allow any of these demons to reach Miranda.

Ryo sliced off the head of yet another male. He jumped up to clear the blast. This was too easy, as if these demons were just fledglings. He focused on Jasmine and tried to speak to her mind, but he couldn't, this too was strange. Perhaps Saban told her not to try and contact him. This would make sense in a way the demons wouldn't be able to trace her. But still none of these fledglings seemed to have the power to track anything. Only ancient demons could do such things.

Gabriele leapt in the air and grabbed the female demon as she tried to escape. Both landed on the ground with a thud. Gabriele quickly grabbed her dagger and embedded it into the neck of the demon. Then she pulled out her pistol and blew the demon's head off. She leapt back into the air to avoid the blast of the demon's soul being destroyed. She landed next to Ryo.

"Something is wrong Ryo," she said, reaching back and grabbing her shotgun. "I can't reach Ryker."

"Nor can I reach Jasmine." Ryo raced forward and sliced off another demon's head. He leapt out of the way from the blast of the demon's soul being destroyed.

After what seemed like an eternity, Michael killed the last of the demons. Michael collapsed on the ground next to Gabriele. "I can't reach Miranda," he said as he tried to catch his breath. Never had they fought so many demon Generals at one time before. Sure they have fought many lesser-demons but not this many Generals.

Ryo jumped up to his feet. "This was a trap, we have to go." The urgency in his voice made both Gabriele and Michael come quickly up to their feet.

"A trap?" Gabriele's heart pounded in her chest.

"These demons were but fledglings. How else could we have defeated this many of them."

"Fuck!!!" Michael screamed.

"Michael…" Gabriele watched as he pounded on a tree.

"I should have seen this, damn it!!" Michael closed his eyes and focused on Miranda. Still he couldn't reach her.

"Let's head back towards the old camp, then we will go in the direction they went," Ryo suggested.

"We have been fighting for many hours now. How will we know which way they went? I can't even get a hold of Saban."

"Michael what if…" Gabriele sat back down on the ground. "What if they are already dead?"

"Don't say that," Michael growled.

"I believe they are not dead." Ryo walked over and pulled Gabriele up to her feet. "But they will be if we don't find them soon."

"Go find my son!!!" Asurul's voice blasted in their minds.

"Ayden." Gabriele looked at Michael and Ryo.

"Fuck!!!" Michael screamed again.

"If he dies I will kill your soul mates myself," Asurul growled.

"All right, let's find Ayden first, then we find the others. Saban will keep them safe." Ryo felt almost ill saying that. But he dare not disobey Asurul.

"What if one of us goes and tries to find the others and the other two go get Ayden, that way Saban will have some help," Gabriele suggested.

"No, damn it, if we split up this will make us weaker and whoever the General in charge of all them knows this," Michael said. "Focus on Ayden, let's find him quickly."

"I can't hone in on Ayden," Gabriele said.

"Then this is a demon's doing." Ryo felt his heart sink. This was a trap and now Jasmine is out there without him to protect her.

"Demon's doing?" Gabriele grabbed his arm.

"A demon has somehow blocked our mental pathways to the others, no doubt an ancient demon's skill."

"No….Ryker….I sent him away, I said he would be safer." Gabriele tried to hold back her tears.

"Ryker is a skilled soldier, Gabriele," Michael added. "He will help Saban protect the women."

"My hunters."

"Ayden!" Gabriele grabbed both Michael and Ryo's arms.

"I feel your worry."

Quadrants to where Ayden was popped into their minds.

"But how was he able to get through the demon's spell?" Gabriele gathered up her daggers.

"He is much stronger than even an ancient General of Hell," Ryo stated. "Asurul must be too, so his threats should not be taken lightly."

"Move it," Michael growled as he took off. Ryo waited for Gabriele then they followed Michael towards Ayden.

 හහහ

Saban slowly made his way through the forest. He couldn't use his demon speed there was no way he could carry all three of them. He looked back to make sure the women were able to keep up. He placed Ryker at the back to ensure the women's safety.

"I can't feel Michael's presence in my mind," Miranda said. She was worried. Michael should have tried to contact them already. "Saban has he tried to contact you?"

"No, we must keep moving." Saban could feel the presence of several demons heading their way.

"Are you ladies able to keep going?" Ryker asked. Being around Saban long enough Ryker knew something was wrong.

"Yes, don't worry about us," Jasmine replied.

"Hunter how will you protect three mortals?" a female voice purred.

Saban came to an abrupt stop. "Ready your weapons." He scanned everywhere and spotted the small blonde-haired woman perched in the tree. "Don't underestimate her, Ryker." Saban kept his eye on the woman as she jumped from tree to tree.

"Stay back." Ryker placed himself in front of the women.

"Shoot for its head Jasmine," Miranda said as she readied Michael's pistol. She looked over and saw that Jasmine already had her pistol up and ready. Miranda leaned back against the tree, she remembered how powerful the recoil was from this gun.

Ryker aimed his pistol at the woman, but just before he shot Saban leapt up and grabbed the woman. Ryker immediately scanned the area around them. "Duck Jasmine." She quickly did and Ryker shot.

A shrill sound of a woman's scream filled the air. Miranda quickly turned and fired. She was thrown back from the gun's recoil and Ryker caught her. A blast knocked Jasmine back. "Damn that pistol got a kick," Ryker said as he checked her for injuries. He looked up and saw Saban slicing the other female's head off. The blast of the demon's soul being destroyed knocked Saban from the tree, but he landed on his feet when he hit the ground.

Miranda went over and helped Jasmine back up to her feet.

"Is everyone all right?" Saban said as he jumped back down.

"Yeah everyone is fine. There are more demons coming isn't there?" Ryker reloaded his pistol.

"Yes, we must move quickly." Saban knew there was no way he could fight the powerful Generals who were closing in on them alone. But he would give everything he had to ensure the safety of these three mortals. The two demons they just fought were but fledglings who were trying to impress their mentors. There were sure to be more of them as well.

"Saban hold on, we will be there as soon as I can meet up with the other hunters." Ayden's voice brought him a measure of calm.

"I will protect them. I have a feeling you won't make it in time. You know the Grand General knows where you are. I swear I will protect the other hunters' soul mates."

"Saban...you are a noble man."

Saban blocked Ayden out of his mind. He looked back at Ryker, Miranda and Jasmine; the other hunters put these three under his protection. Could he protect them?

"Don't underestimate us, Saban," Ryker commented when he saw the worried look in Saban's eyes. "I will get back to Gabriele, she needs me."

"We will fight, Saban. Nothing will keep me from Ryo," Jasmine added.

"Just tell us what you need us to do. I survived Hell, killing a couple of demons is within my capabilities. I have Michael to go back to."

Saban saw the strength and resolve of all of them. "Okay, let's get some distance between us and those demons. We will stand a better chance if we can somehow get them to separate from each other. Knowing a demon, he or she will not want to share their prize with anyone. Let's give them a little more time to squabble with each other."

"Ladies you heard him, let's move it," Ryker said, grabbing the weapon packs from the women. Though they protested a little, Ryker knew they would move faster this way.

Chapter 12

"My hunters, go find your soul mates." Ayden squeezed Emily's hand. A strong presence was heading towards him. It must be the Grand General and his helpers. He had brought Diane and Shelly to the nearest hospital hoping that the large number of mortals in one place would deter the demons from pursuing them. Now he felt his hunters' fear for their soul mates. How could he ask them to risk everything to protect him? After all the years these three have given him, their loyalty, strength, and compassion. How could he ask that they risk more?

"Ayden, we can't leave you alone," Michael's voice filled his mind.

"I order you to help the others. I am going to lead this General away from here."

"Ayden, your safety is our biggest concern."

"Gabriele, you know Ryker is your biggest concern and right now he needs you. Now go!"

Ayden closed his mind off to them. He only hoped that they would obey him. "Stay here for a moment." He caressed Emily's face. He walked down the hallway of the hospital and out to the parking lot. It was late at night and everything was very quiet.

"Father, if you can hear me, I gave the hunters the order to return to the others."

"Ayden, no." Asurul's voice seemed strained as if he was in pain.

"Father, the choice is mine. I stand by myself or I die. At least my hunters will be able to protect that which is most precious to them. I couldn't live with their pain on my conscience should any harm fall upon the others."

"Ayden...you can't face the General who is hunting you. I trained Tryton..."

"I am stronger than you give me credit for. I am not a little boy anymore, father."

"You will always be my little boy, Ayden."

Ayden choked back his tears. He could feel his father's love for him. It amazed him that a man, who knew nothing of love until he met Isa, could be so passionate in the love he gave both of them.

"No matter what happens, please know I love you and mother very much."

"Ayden you can't face Tryton alone. Now call back the hunters to aid you."

"Goodbye father."

Ayden closed his mind to Asurul. This Tryton was clever. The trap he had designed was very well planned. But no matter, he would face this Tryton alone.

"Ayden, are you all right?"

"Emily…" Ayden watched her walk over to him. He had to get her away from here too, but how?

"What's wrong?"

"We have to leave now." Ayden scooped her up into his arms and held her tight to him. She wrapped her arms around his neck.

"Thank you for helping my friends."

"You needn't thank me Emily."

"But I want to." She raised her lips to his and kissed him. Her body demanded she entice him to make love to her. But her mind told her now wasn't the time to think of such things.

Ayden could see every erotic image that raced through her mind. His cock hardened seeing these images. He almost growled smelling the scent of her arousal as he held their fiery kiss. His tongue probed deeply into her mouth as hers did the same.

"Emily," he sighed as he deepened their kiss. He wanted her so badly at this moment. When she let out a little moan and intensified her kiss, he could barely contain his need for her.

He had to get them to safety. Though he wanted her with every fiber of his being he would have to wait to claim her. He slowly moved his lips from hers. That was precisely what he wanted to do, claim her as his. There was no more fear, no more doubt, she was his, all his. There could be no other for him. That look of lust and love in her eyes as he gazed lovingly into her face drove him to distraction.

"We must go Emily."

He looked to make sure no one was watching then he took to the sky. He had to put distance between him and Tryton. Emily's friends would be safe then.

Emily looked out over the night sky. The stars were so bright from up here. The wind caressed her skin and the warmth of Ayden's body made her feel safe. "Where are we going?"

"To Florida or maybe further."

"Florida…and you are planning to fly us there?"

"Of course." He smiled down at her.

"Something is really wrong isn't it?"

"At this moment…" he gazed into her eyes, "nothing is wrong."

ജ്ഞ

"Where does he think he is going?" Tryton paced back and forth. He was nearly where Ayden was now that asshole decided to take off. Even more peculiar was that those demon hunters weren't following him.

"Now what Grand General?" Alma smirked. These last two days being by his side were trying to say the least. He teased her at every opportunity. But damn it, she loved the bastard and just being by his side was enough for her.

"Shut up bitch," Tryton growled.   "Why would Ayden do that?" Tryton rethought everything.

"Perhaps he sent Emily with the hunters hoping to lead you away from her." Jaxon offered.

"Ah, perhaps." Tryton smiled. "Tell half of the Generals I sent hunting for the mortals to head towards the hunters. By time they reach them, those mortals should be dead anyways."

"Yes Tryton," Jaxon took off. He wanted to get on Tryton's good side just in case his plan worked and Lasax made him second in command.

"The rest of you, we will pursue Ayden. But first find me some mortal women, I want to have some fun. Let Ayden think his plan is working, then we will strike."

"Will these two do?" Alma dragged in two young women.

"Ah yes. Where did you find these tasty morsels?"

"This is their apartment we are…well let's say borrowing." Alma threw the women down towards Tryton's feet.

"What are you going to do to them?" Alma smiled. She became more aroused by the moment. That delicious look on his face made her pussy wet.

"Make them fall in love with me." Tryton helped the women to their feet. "Mmm, so young, so beautiful," he said, caressing their cheeks. He weaved his spell on them and soon both women began caressing him.

He led them over to the bed. "Take your clothes off and wait for me." He slowly took his shirt off all the while watching the two women undress.

"Alma care to watch?" He smiled at her. Knowing he could make Alma suffer always added to his enjoyment.

Alma sat on the chair that was across from the bed. She had already taken off her pants and now she sat there leisurely stroking her clit. Looking at Tryton's beautiful body drove her crazy with want.

Tryton climbed onto the bed and both women began caressing and kissing him. "Eager aren't you," he purred, enjoying their touches.

Alma watched the women kiss, suck and lick every part of Tryton's body. They were so enraptured with him they would do anything he asked. She knew Tryton would ask much of these two mortal women. She stroked her clit faster and faster as she watched one of the women suck on Tryton's cock. She longed to taste Tryton, but he was picky in which demon he decided to bed. The moans and sounds of sex filled the room, making Alma hungry. She groaned when Tryton stuck his cock deep into one woman while the other caressed his balls with her tongue. Alma moved her fingers faster and harder in a circular motion over her clit, watching Tryton's cock go in and out of the mortal's pussy. The faster Tryton thrust, the faster Alma stroked. Her whole body quivered when Tryton locked eyes with her. He roared his orgasm, causing Alma's body to quake from her climax.

Tryton used both women for several hours and Alma watched every moment. She knew he took delight in tormenting her which in a strange way made it all that much sweeter for her. Any other male demon treated her this way and she would have torn them apart by now, but Tryton, oh, she would do anything, be anything for him.

"That was interesting," he said as he got dressed. "Now my finale."

Alma watched as he closed his eyes and within seconds the two mortal women slowly walked over toward the window. Alma slowly rose up as the women climbed out onto the ledge. She rushed towards the window just as both women jumped, falling twelve stories to the ground below. "How did you do that? I would have had to physically thrown them out the window."

"Mind games are easy on the weak willed." Tryton signaled for the rest of the Generals to prepare to move out.

"Tryton…" Alma hurried to him. "Take my body as you did those mortals."

"You want to end up a splattered mess on the ground?"

"You know what I mean. Fuck me, Tryton."

Tryton started to laugh. "Mortals I fuck for sport." He looked at her with disgust. "You are not worthy to have me. But don't take it personal Alma, very few female demons are."

Alma wanted to scream from the frustration she felt. "Damn you Tryton," she growled, watching him walk away. He kept her so close to him only to torture her.

Chapter 13

Saban stayed on alert as the other's rested. They moved more quickly than he thought they would. The women were exhausted, but Ryker looked to be in okay shape and he too was standing guard over the women. The air crackled with evil energy. Saban could feel it and judging by how on edge the others were it looked, they felt it too.

"Here have some water," Ryker said, handing his canteen to Miranda.

"Have you contacted Gabriele yet?" she asked.

"No, but Saban said Ayden contacted him. He said help was coming."

"Do you think…Michael and the others are still alive?" Miranda didn't want to think of the possibility Michael was dead, but not hearing from him for this long was making her worry.

"No, I don't think they're dead," Ryker said, handing the canteen to Jasmine. "I would sense if Gabriele was dead."

"Ryker come here please," Saban called out.

"They are alive, Miranda." He smiled at her before he headed over towards Saban.

"I need to talk to you alone for a moment. Miranda and Jasmine stay right there." Saban walked a little ways out into the woods with Ryker right behind him. He looked out over nature's beauty. "There are several ancient demons heading towards us. I was hoping by now they would have started to fight with one another, but it looks like that's not going to happen. When they catch up, which shouldn't be too much longer, I am going to fight all of them alone."

"What?!"

"I want you to take the women and head up that small mountain." Saban pointed to it. "I will try to keep them busy."

"I don't see what that will accomplish. We can help you fight the demons."

"When I scouted ahead earlier I spotted a cave on the eastern side of that mountain." Saban waited a moment while Ryker took out his binoculars and looked for the cave. "There you will take the women. It will provide you some sort of cover and you only have to fight whatever demon that gets pass me on one front."

Ryker slowly lowered his binoculars. All his training told him this was the best course of action. The cave would provide them with cover and they could blast any demon that tried to enter. "What about you?"

"I swore to Gabriele, Michael and Ryo, I would keep you all safe."

"You can't take on all those demons yourself."

"I know, but I will buy you time." Saban walked back towards the women.

Ryker stood there silent for a moment. Saban was going to die protecting them. It was as if he had accepted this already. And yet Saban showed no fear or remorse for his decision.

"Ryker we must move out," Saban called out.

Ryker took a deep breath then headed back towards the others. He grabbed the weapons packs and took his place behind the women.

"Do you need help carrying any of that?" Jasmine asked.

"No, I am fine." Ryker smiled at her. His thoughts kept drifting to Gabriele. Was she alive? Would he really feel if she had died? In his heart he believed that he would, this gave him hope. He wished he would hear her sweet voice in his head, so that he would know that she still lived. No matter what he felt he would fight until his last breath to protect the women and to get back to Gabriele.

They walked for a couple more miles; the small mountain's base was only another mile or so ahead.

"Ryker you remember what I told you?" Saban said running back towards him.

"Yes,"

"Then go." Saban charged back into the forest.

"Where is he going?" Jasmine asked.

"Come on we got to get up to that cave." Ryker sprinted forward and looked back to make sure the women were following. With the heavy backpack it slowed him, making it easy for the women to keep up.

Once they reached the base Ryker started climbing. "Be careful," he called down. He kept looking down to make sure they were keeping up. He reached the first ridge and helped the women over it. He allowed them to catch their breath for a moment. They heard a loud boom.

"Saban is fighting those demons alone, isn't he?" Jasmine asked.

"Yes."

"We can't let him do that."

"We have to get to that cave." Ryker looked up and saw the cave wasn't too much further up.

"Ryker we can't let him fight all those demons alone," Jasmine repeated.

"We have no choice Jasmine. Now let's move it." Ryker didn't feel right letting Saban fight those demons alone either, but there was really no other way.

They climbed up to the next ridge. Ryker helped the women up. Thankfully this is where the cave was. He didn't think the women could physically take much more. He escorted them in the cave and set out the weapons. They had three shotguns, three regular pistols, Michael's pistol, one rifle, several clips of ammo for each, and two grenades.

"Grab a weapon and get ready to use it." Ryker grabbed his rifle and headed out of the cave. From his vantage point he could see into the forest. Saban looked to be fighting six ancient demons, though Ryker's view was somewhat blocked from the trees. He attached his scope to his rifle, kicked out the bipod and then lay down on the ground. He steadied himself as he looked through the scope. The demons were moving at incredible speed, getting a shot in would prove difficult, but he had to help Saban somehow. He focused and aimed his shots carefully he couldn't afford to hit Saban by mistake. He fired off a couple of rounds managing to hit one of the male demons. This bought Saban a little time. Saban immediately raced towards the wounded and stunned demon. Ryker followed him in the scope. He fired another round hitting the other male demon who was pursuing Saban. Ryker took a deep breath. Saban managed to kill the wounded demon but was thrown back from the blast of its soul being destroyed.

"Damn it," Ryker muttered. The rest of the demons charged at Saban. Ryker managed to shoot two. But these demons were fast. Two grabbed Saban and leapt into the air. Ryker managed to shoot one, freeing one of Saban's arms. Saban wrestled with the remaining demon then tossed him to the ground as they descended. Ryker could see that Saban was wounded. But still he fought. Saban killed another demon, this time leaping above the blast. That left four more. One of the demons tackled Saban, but he managed to throw him off. Ryker noticed Saban was slow to get back up.

"Hold on," Ryker whispered. He took aim at another male shooting him in the head. Saban charged and sliced the male's head off. But he was too slow to avoid the blast this time and was thrown. The last three charged at Saban all at once. Ryker managed to shoot one of the males, but the other male and female grabbed Saban. The trees blocked Ryker's view so he couldn't take the shot. He turned his attention back at the other male; he shot him again forcing him away from where Saban was. Ryker gasped, seeing the two other demons being thrown back, followed by a large billow of smoke. He heard the roar of the demons echo through the forest.

Ryker quickly got back up and headed back into the cave. "Get ready," he said to the women.

"What about Saban?" Jasmine asked as she grabbed a shotgun.

"He is dead." Ryker said, grabbing Michael's pistol. Now wasn't the time to let emotions cloud his judgment.

"Oh no…" Miranda held back her tears as she grabbed a shotgun and aimed it towards the opening.

"There are three of them left." Ryker checked their weapons to make sure all of them were loaded. "Jasmine, when your weapon runs out of ammo, you will be in charge of reloading the weapons. You will hand us the weapons that are fully reloaded."

"Okay." Jasmine cocked her shotgun.

"Your hunter is dead mortals," a male demon cackled.

Evity positioned herself at the side of the cave. She knew that mortal man was the one who shot them as they fought Saban. These two arrogant male demons wouldn't give the mortal credit; she didn't intend to make that mistake.

The sound of gunfire rang out and the first male was blown back away from the cave's entrance.

Ryker continued to fire at the males as they kept trying to come into the cave. Though bloody, they kept coming. "Aim for his head this time Miranda." Ryker focused and as Miranda shot at the male again, he aimed for the head and blew it clean off the demon's body. Ryker placed himself in front of the women and took the brunt of the blast.

"Two more," Jasmine said as she immediately went back to reloading. Their ammo was quickly running out.

The other male was a bit faster, but they managed to keep him at bay. What Ryker didn't like was the fact that the female hasn't tried to come in. "Save the last of the shotgun shells, Jasmine."

"Okay." Jasmine set the shotgun aside.

"Miranda hit him in the chest area; I will go for his head again." Ryker stood up and readied his shotgun. Miranda fired and Ryker quickly shot at the male's head, blowing it off. Again he covered the women.

"How much more ammo do we got?" Ryker cocked back the shotgun. He had only two more bullets in this one.

"That's it, just this last shotgun."

Ryker handed Miranda the shotgun with the two bullets left and he grabbed the fully loaded one. He saw the two grenades sitting on the ground. He stood up and prepared himself for the female General.

"Well I see you managed to kill my two eager male companions," Evity called out. "So that you know mortals, I was the one who cut off that demon hunter's head."

"You bitch," Miranda growled.

"Steady yourself." Ryker grabbed Miranda's arm.

"Ah, don't worry Miranda when I take your life you can be with Michael again."

"He is not dead!"

"Don't be too sure about that."

"Miranda don't let her words get to you." Ryker grabbed her arm again.

"Jasmine wouldn't you like to see Ryo again?"

"Go back to Hell bitch."

Evity's laughter enraged them. "Ummm Ryker, I am going to fuck you before I send you off to Purgatory to be with Gabriele again."

"You are a clever demon, but I know you are full of shit. Keep telling us your lies, demon, you are wasting your time."

Evity growled then dashed into the cave. Miranda fired but missed. Ryker charged at Evity, she was too fast to aim at so he would just get up close and personal. He fired one shot grazing her arm. She grabbed the shotgun and ripped it from Ryker's hand. She snapped the gun in two.

"Now what mortal?"

Ryker got ready to fight her. She leapt at him and knocked him to the ground. She pinned him under her. "So beautiful," she purred, licking his face. Ryker struggled but Evity was extremely strong.

"Get off him," Miranda charged at her with the empty shotgun, but before she could hit Evity she was thrown to the back of the cave.

"Stay back," Ryker yelled. His eyes locked on the grenades. He had to reach them. He would blow this bitch up, of course he would have to die with her, but at least the women would be safe.

"Your body pleases me." Evity looked over his strong arms and chest. "I think I will keep you as a plaything for awhile."

"Get off him bitch," Jasmine cried out.

Miranda's eyes widened when a large dark-haired man entered the cave. "Not another one," Miranda whispered. But to her surprise the strange man grabbed Evity and pulled her off Ryker.

"Tasmos," Evity growled as she kicked him away from her.

Ryker hurried back to the women. He grabbed the two grenades and placed one in each hand. He had his fingers positioned to pop the pins.

"Who is that?" Jasmine asked.

"An Archangel." Ryker watched Evity circle Tasmos. The cave wasn't that big and there was little room for Tasmos to maneuver.

"What are you planning on doing with those?" Miranda said, looking at the grenades in Ryker's hands.

"Plan B."

"I won't let you do that Ryker," Jasmine said, placing her hand on one of the grenades. Miranda placed her hand on the other.

Ryker looked at the two women. "There is no other way."

Both women squeezed his hands tighter and then looked at the battle in front of them. Ryker knew he could easily shake them off, but their gesture touched him.

Tasmos circled Evity. He was drawn here when he felt Saban fall. He had watched the mortals battle with the demons so bravely. He was compelled to help the mortal mate of Gabriele.

Evity kept her eye on the dagger strapped to Tasmos' side. She would have to get that dagger. But Tasmos was an ancient Archangel. She would not make the mistake of underestimating him. They continued their dance, she would lunge at him and he would throw her off. He was trying to get her out of this cave. She pretended to run for the cave's entrance knowing he would follow. Just before she got there she turned as fast as she could then leapt at him knocking him to the ground. Without hesitation she grabbed his dagger.

"Die angel," Evity laughed. She lifted the dagger up high in the air then just as she went to plunge it into his chest, her hand was shot off. She screamed and quickly leapt off Tasmos. She looked to the cave entrance.

"Huntress…."she roared.

"Gabriele," Tasmos said as he got up and grabbed Evity. He nodded his head towards her then took to the sky with Evity tightly in his grasp.

"Ryker…" Gabriele lowered her weapon. Her relief seeing him alive made her body shake.

Michael and Ryo leapt up to the cliff. "I told you not to get ahead of us." They both looked to the back of the cave and saw Ryker standing in front of the women with grenades in his hands.

"It's over for now Ryker." Gabriele slowly walked over to him.

Ryker couldn't believe his eyes. Gabriele was alive, a little beaten up but otherwise okay. He lowered the grenades and slowly put them on the ground. Miranda and Jasmine ran over to Michael and Ryo.

"You were a little late, huntress." Ryker said, pulling her into his arms.

"You are okay." She started to cry.

"Thank you Tasmos," she whispered, holding Ryker tighter. She breathed in the scent of him. "Thank you." If Tasmos hadn't shown up when he did, or if she didn't show when she did…Gabriele didn't want to think about it.

"Where is Ayden?" Miranda asked as she basked in the warmth of Michael's arms.

"I don't know." Michael held her tightly to him.

"What? You don't know where he is? I thought you knew instinctively where to find him."

"He has closed his mind to us. I think he is trying to protect us."

"But, he can't fight all those demons alone."

"I know, Miranda, I know." Michael held her closer.

Ayden was out there somewhere and they had to find him, though each of them wanted nothing more than to stay in their soul mates arms, there was little time. They tried to figure out where he might have gone. But he could have gone anywhere. He had the ability to fly like an Archangel which meant he could cover a lot of ground very quickly.

"Where is Saban?" Gabriele asked as she looked around for him. Gabriele looked over at the somber faces of Miranda, Jasmine and Ryker.

"He died...protecting us." Miranda started to cry. Now that everything was over for now, the depths of Saban's sacrifice were felt by all three of them.

Gabriele looked into Ryker's face, she could see the sadness in his eyes. "Where?"

Ryker grabbed her hand. The others followed them into the forest. All that was left was a pile of ash. Gabriele grabbed a jar from her backpack and carefully gathered some of the ash. Ryo and Michael bowed their heads and had a moment of silence for their fallen comrade.

Ryker stared at the pile of ash. If only he could have got a couple more shots off, maybe he could have saved Saban. But another thought nagged at him. This is what happens when a hunter died. Would this be all that was left of Gabriele if demons got her?

"Ryker, you tried your best?" Jasmine gently grabbed his arm.

"Did I?" He looked to the ground.

"Yes, you did."

"Thank you." He smiled and patted her hand. She went back over to Ryo.

"Gabriele, is this how all hunters die?"

"Yes."

"I don't want to ever see you like this." Ryker turned from the ashes.

"You won't."

"But you can't guarantee it."

"There are no guarantees in life, Ryker." She wrapped her arms around his waist and snuggled against his back.

Michael grabbed Miranda's hand and walked away from the group a little ways. "Are you all right?" he asked, running his hands over her body.

"I am all right. Ryker tried so hard to help Saban and if it wasn't for him, we wouldn't have made it."

"Then I owe a debt I can never repay."

"I can't stop thinking about Saban. He knew he was going to die, he had to known it. Then I see that pile of ash and I can't stop thinking that might have been you lying there." Miranda started to cry.

"Shhh, it's okay." He stroked her hair gently as he held her to him.

"Michael," Gabriele called out.

He and Miranda went back to the others. "We have to find Ayden," Ryo said, holding Jasmine's hand tightly. "Ryker," he turned to him. "I owe you for protecting Jasmine."

"As well as I for protecting Miranda."

"They helped, they were strong. So you don't owe me. Besides, it is Tasmos and Saban you should thank." A hush fell over the group.

"All right Ryo, you said we have to find Ayden." Jasmine broke the silence.

"We?"

"Do you think I am going to let you out of my sight?"

Ryo smiled at her. "Knowing Ayden he has led the Grand General away from here. So let's head towards the East. All we can do is hope he opens his mind back up to us."

"Leave your minds open to me. Ryker and I will catch up when we can." Gabriele knew she couldn't carry Ryker. Now that Saban was gone…she hoped his death was a clean one and that he didn't suffer.

"All right, let's go." Michael picked up Miranda and took off. Ryo grabbed Jasmine and followed after him.

"We need to get to the airport or train station." Gabriele said, grabbing Ryker's hand.

Chapter 14

Ayden landed and gently set Emily down. Emily looked around at the beautiful forest. "You like Nature don't you?" she asked.

"Yes, I feel at peace surrounded by Nature's beauty." Ayden did a quick scan, for now they were safe.

"Tell me more about you." Emily sat down on the soft grass. The sun was starting to set and the evening chill had begun to fill the air.

"What would you like to know?" Ayden gathered some firewood then rubbed his hands together and held them over the wood, making the wood instantly catch fire.

"You left off when your parents died." Emily welcomed Ayden's embrace as he sat down behind her and drew her closer to him.

"About a week after my father died, both my parents came to me."

"As ghost?"

"No, more like angels. They told me that my test was to begin. At first it seemed simple enough, I was only to find my true love. But..."

"But it wasn't simple at all was it?"

"No, the first woman I thought loved me, prove not to. She only desired me. She became so possessive of me she murdered her friend."

"Why?"

"She believed that we were sleeping together. I didn't know what to feel or do when she was taken to prison. My mother put me to sleep so I wouldn't have to feel anything. When I awoke ten years later…"

"Years!"

"Yes, years, when I awoke I saw three men guarding me. My father explained to me that these men were demon hunters and they were there to protect me. Well, I grew to love my hunters as brothers, but one by one they died protecting me against the demons. Each time I failed a woman, my mother put me to sleep and each time three hunters would stand guard over me. When I awoke, I would see new hunters who had replaced the ones that were killed. And my pain would be renewed. Each time one of my hunters dies, I feel as though I lost a member of my family."

"Ayden, I am so sorry to hear about your loss. But why would you think you failed those women?"

"Because I couldn't be want they wanted."

"No, they couldn't be what you needed." Emily drew his arms tighter around her. She couldn't imagine what it would be like to suffer so much loss. "How long has this gone on?"

"I have lived for over four hundred years."

Emily came up to her knees and turned to face him. "Four hundred years." She gently caressed his cheek. "And yet you are so open and kind to everyone. Four hundred years…"

"You were worth the wait Emily." Ayden nuzzled his cheek against her hand.

Tears fell from her eyes. She didn't know what to say. Ayden pulled her to him and kissed her deeply. "I want to make love to you," he whispered as he laid her down gently in the grass. He couldn't wait any longer to make love to her. Emily reached up and pulled his shirt up, he helped her remove it.

"You are so beautiful," she said, letting her hands wander over his chest.

Ayden slowly unbuttoned her blouse then gently moved the fabric aside. He lowered and trailed kisses down her stomach. His hair felt like silk against her skin as he moved lower and lower. He paused and started unbuttoning her jeans.

"Wait," she said.

He moved himself back up and looked into her eyes. "Don't you want me?"

"More than anything, but…"

"But what?"

"You are so beautiful and I…am so ordinary." She grabbed a handful of his silky blond hair. "I am not exactly…well…in the best shape and I don't know if once you see my body if…"

Ayden placed his fingers on her lips. "You are the most beautiful woman I have ever seen." He stood up and helped her to her feet. He walked her over to a small pond. "I want you to see what I see." He waved his hand over the pond to calm the water. Emily looked into the water and saw her reflection. Her skin glowed with radiance, her body looked lush and tempting, and her eyes were alive and seemed to dance. She reached her hand up and touched her face. It was her, but….

"This is how you see me?"

"Yes, you are looking at yourself through my eyes."

"Ayden…" She turned around and wrapped her arms around him. He scooped her up and carried her back over to the grass.

"Let me see your beautiful body." He helped her remove her clothing. He could still see her hesitation. He slowly lowered her down to the grass. His hands caressed her body. He took his time wanting to feel every inch of her. His fingers ran through the soft curls that covered her pussy. Her scent intoxicated him. He looked into her eyes. Slowly he lowered his lips to hers. His kiss was hungry and urgent, his body full of need.

"Ayden," she sighed when he cupped her breast firmly in his hand.

He lowered his body down and took her nipple into his mouth and gently suckled as his hand continued kneading the other breast. Emily ran her hands through his hair as he suckled. Her whole body burned with desire. All sorts of delicious images filled her mind, everything she wanted to do to him.

"Mmm, do anything you want to me," he moaned, he could see all the erotic images that raced through her mind. He traveled kisses down her belly and paused when he reached her pussy. He breathed in the sweet smell of her. Slowly he parted her pussy lips as delicately as someone opening the bud of a flower. He blew softly across her clit and felt her thighs quiver.

"Ayden," she panted.

He let his tongue flick across her clit then he latched his mouth onto her. He licked, sucked and kissed at her pussy as though it was a succulent piece of fruit. He groaned as his cock became harder and harder the more he ate her. He almost growled when she ran her fingers through his hair, pushing him closer to her as her body bucked and she cried his name. He stuck two of his fingers deeply in her as she climaxed. He leisurely continued to lick at her as he drove his fingers in and out. He added a third, then a fourth finger, stretching her. He latched his mouth back on to her clit and sucked gently.

"Ayden, ahh, mmm," Emily started to squirm. Her orgasm was so powerful, she began fucking his fingers, wanting them to go deeper. "Ayden please."

Ayden licked at her clit one last time then reached down and removed his pants. He spread her legs and slowly positioned himself between them.

"Wait, I want to touch your body first."

Ayden lay down next to her. "My body is yours to do with as you please," he said softly. He enjoyed the fire in her eyes as her hands traveled down his body.

Emily let her hands linger over every muscle line of his body. The hardness yet softness of him felt wonderful. The sheer perfection of his body was arousing. And the scent of him was heavenly.

"I don't know how much more I can take Emily," he moaned.

Her hands went to his large, hard cock. Slowly she stroked him, loving the feel of him in her hands. She let one hand slip down to his balls and gently kneaded them.

"Emily…please…let me have you."

Emily let her hand slowly go up his shaft then she let her thumb rub just under the head. She used his precum to lube her thumb as she continued to stroke over, around and under the head of his cock.

"No more," he growled, pulling her to him.

He rolled her over and pinned her under him. He kissed her as he slowly let his cock fill her. Her pussy sheathed his cock snuggly. He groaned and buried his cock to the hilt in her. He thrust hard yet slowly into her as he held his fiery kiss. He could feel her hands in his hair as he continued to ride her. He arched up when he felt her pussy walls clamp down on his cock, squeezing, milking him.

"Ayden," she sighed, running her hands up his chest.

He sat back on his heels and lifted her up. He cupped her ass as he drove his cock into her over and over. Emily wrapped her arms around his shoulders and pulled him closer, wanting to feel his body rub against hers.

"Ah…ooh, Emily…" he cried out. He continued to thrust deeply into her as he came. He wrapped his arms around her and held her tightly to him as he enjoyed the afterglow of his orgasm.

He laid them down and held her in his arms. Never had he felt so complete before. "I love you, Emily," he whispered as he nuzzled his cheek against the top of her head.

She lay there quietly for a moment then lifted herself up a little so she could look into his golden eyes. "I love you, Ayden." She was sure of this now.

Ayden's heart felt as though it could burst. The honesty of her words could be seen in her eyes. He kissed her softly then held her tightly to him. He could lie like this forever, but he could sense the demons catching up to them.

Chapter 15

Tryton could feel Ayden's presence. "What a fool." He chuckled. Why would Ayden pick such a remote spot to challenge him? "Listen up you peons," Tryton's voice boomed. "That son of the traitor Asurul is just a few miles ahead of us and it seems he has decided to stop running from me. I don't want him getting away this time. Our Master wants Ayden's soul and he shall have it." Tryton roared loud followed by the other demons.

He positioned the ten Generals that were with him so that they would surround Ayden. There was no way that asshole was escaping this time. He sent a fledgling demon out to scout ahead of them. He still didn't sense the hunters anywhere near them. So there was no one left to protect Ayden. This brought a smile to Tryton's face. He knew he was more powerful than any of these other Generals here. Ayden and his hunters had already destroyed some of Hell's most powerful Generals over the course of Ayden's existence. Even Manus, Lasax's most vicious General fell by the hands of Ayden. Tryton wasn't as cocky as those other Generals had been. He would not underestimate Ayden. After those other ten Generals weaken Ayden, he would come in for the kill. It was a perfect plan.

Excitement filled him as he waited for the fledgling to come back. His goal was so near completion. Lasax would be most pleased.

"Tryton." The female demon hurried to him.

"Well what did you find?"

"Ayden and his woman are two miles ahead. He must have felt my presence, yet he made no attempt to leave."

"He has his woman with him?"

"Yes sir."

"Very good." He stroked her hair gently. He smiled hearing Alma growl. Oh did he love teasing that demon bitch.

"All right my fellow demons it's time to attack." Tryton took off running.

Alma was right behind him. She was determined to kill Ayden for Tryton, maybe this would make her worthy of his love.

The other demons headed out to their designated positions too. An excitement raced through all of them. Finally Lasax would have Ayden's soul, and the one who actually killed Ayden would most certainly be rewarded.

ഔഔഔ

Michael and Ryo both froze at the same time when the quadrants for where Ayden was popped into their minds.

"What's wrong?" Miranda asked, looking up into Michael's face. They had stopped so Gabriele and Ryker could catch up; they were taking an airplane and meeting them in Atlanta.

"Ayden has finally opened his mind to us."

"That's good, isn't it?"

"Yes, it is." Michael smiled down at her.

"My hunters, where is Saban?"

"He was killed protecting the others." Michael could feel Ayden's sadness.

"I want you all to know that I can never repay you for what you have done for me. And that I have loved you all like family."

"Why are you talking as if you are never going to see us again? We are not too far away from where you are, just hang on."

"The demons will be here any moment; you will not make it in time, goodbye my hunters." Ayden closed his mind to them again.

"No, we can't let him give up," Ryo said.

"If the demons are upon him already, we will not make it in time, even if we leave right now." Michael didn't know what to do.

"Then you two go and try to reach him. Ayden is strong he might hold off the demons for awhile," Miranda said.

"I can't leave you alone."

"Nor can I leave Jasmine."

"Go, Miranda and I will be fine. You have to try and help him."

"Yeah and you're wasting time standing here arguing with us, we will tell Gabriele that you have gone ahead when she gets here," Miranda added.

"That's right, Gabriele will be here soon, so see we will be fine, now go."

Ryo raced over to Jasmine and kissed her then took off. Michael did the same to Miranda.

"Do you think they will be able to reach Ayden in time?" Jasmine asked.

"No, but they have to at least try."

⁂⁂⁂

Ayden stood there silently. Another one of his hunters was dead. Saban, he barely got a chance to know this newest hunter. But the brief time he did talk with him, he knew Saban was a good man.

"What's wrong?" Emily said, grabbing his arm.

"Saban is dead."

"Oh no, I am so sorry." She didn't know what else to say. She wrapped her arms around him and held him tightly, wishing she could do more to ease his pain.

Ayden held her for a moment, but that was all the time he could allow himself to take comfort from her. The demons were closing in on them.

"Emily, about ten demon Generals are headed toward us and should be here any moment. I am not sure that I can defeat that many of them alone. I will try until my last breath to protect you." There was no time to morn Saban; he had to focus to protect Emily.

"Let me help you somehow."

"I need you to stay clear of the battle, but this might prove impossible since I feel them surrounding us." He turned toward her. "I love you Emily, and I am sorry because of my love for you, you are probably going to...." He couldn't bring himself to say it. " I should have never revealed myself to you."

"Shh…" She wrapped her arms tighter around him. "These few moments I spent with you were some of the happiest moments of my life and I wouldn't have traded them for anything. Whatever happens let it." She looked up into those beautiful golden eyes of his. "If we die today, then we will be together in the next life."

Ayden choked back his tears. "Yes we will," his voice shook. Her love and acceptance of him was beyond anything he could have ever hoped for. He squeezed her hand then brought her hand up to his lips and softly kissed it. "Stand over there and stay right there, I need to know where you are at all times" He watched Emily go over by a group of trees. He readied himself for battle. He would give everything he had to protect her. He decided if it looked like he was going to be defeated he would kill her, so she wouldn't be left in the hands of the demons. He didn't even want to imagine what they would do to her.

"Grab the pistol I gave you to use and stand back." His hand blades slowly emerged as he prepared himself for battle. There was no more running, no more hiding; he would take a stand against these monsters. Let Lasax send his minions to take his soul. His only regret was Emily had to be here, and that Saban had to lose his life protecting him. Hell that so many hunters' lives were lost protecting him. He had to clear his thoughts and focus. He would have to use everything Asurul taught him. He felt the demons closing in. Ayden growled and got into his battle stance. Let them come, he was ready for them.

Chapter 16

Tryton slowly climbed up the tree, he perched himself on a branch and gazed out over the battlefield. A clearing in the middle of the woods, what a fool Ayden was. He would have been better to go deeper into the forest where he might have used the trees as cover.

He looked over Ayden, trying to find a glimpse of Asurul in him. Ayden's beauty rivaled that of Prolo's, the same couldn't be said about Asurul. There wasn't the same darkness in Ayden's eyes, or bloodlust in his heart as Asurul's. This man before him was ready to fight, ready to kill, but only to protect his woman. Asurul would kill any man who he believed was an enemy, or of course if Lasax ordered him to kill. Asurul would kill without question or remorse. But Tryton couldn't see any of these qualities in Ayden.

"Huh, Asurul it seems your woman has influenced your son too much," Tryton whispered.

He looked over to Emily. She stood beside a group of trees with a handgun gripped in her hands. He let his eyes wander over the rather average-looking woman. "This is your soul mate Ayden?" Tryton scoffed. He figured that Ayden's woman would have been a beauty beyond compare, not some average-looking mortal woman. Tryton was a bit disappointed, he'd planned to take Ayden's woman once he had killed him. Oh, he would still rape and torture the mortal woman, but now he would just have to kill her when he was done.

"You look nothing like your father, Ayden," Tryton shouted.

Ayden quickly looked up at Tryton perched in a tree. "Come down here."

"In due time, but first I want to see how well you hold up against the others. Huh, your stance is similar to Asurul's. Did he teach you how to use those blades?"

"My father taught me well." Ayden clicked his hand blades together.

"He taught me well too, boy." Tryton let his blades emerge as he smiled wickedly at Ayden. Then he gave the signal for the others to attack.

Ayden spun around and saw the demons coming at him from every angle. There were ten of them all approaching him. He glanced over at Emily, she had her pistol raised and ready to shoot anything that came near her. "That's my girl," Ayden whispered.

"Son of Asurul, would you like to know more about your father?" Tryton called out.

Ayden tried to ignore Tryton so he could focus on the demons charging at him. "Emily hold on to something," he cried out. She quickly wrapped her arms around a tree. Ayden concentrated his energy. "Ahhhya!!!" he yelled as a blast of energy radiated from his body knocking all the demons down and back.

"Oh, impressive." Tryton clapped.

Ayden wasted no time, he quickly charged at the first demon, a large dark-haired male. Ayden embedded his blade into the male's stomach and lifted him up, causing the blade to slice up, spilling the demon's insides. Ayden pulled the blade out then spun around and decapitated the demon. He leapt up avoiding the blast but using it to his advantage to knock back the female who was coming up behind him.

"Come on, hurt the bastard," Tryton yelled at the others.

Ayden's attention quickly went towards Emily when he heard her gunfire. He raced over and kicked the male demon that was approaching her. He grabbed her and jumped into the tree. "Stay here for now." He gently caressed her face then jump back down. He hurried over to another male demon but just as he got there, a female demon jumped on his back.

"No," Emily whispered. She watched another demon male lunge at Ayden. She climbed down from the tree and took aim at the female on Ayden's back. She fired twice making the female leap off Ayden and head for her. "Oh shit." Emily lifted her pistol and waited.

Ayden threw the male off him and kicked the other away. He rushed back to Emily and grabbed the female. He pinned her to the ground and quickly sliced her head off. He bolted to Emily and covered her, taking the brunt of the blast. He kissed the top of her head and charged back out there.

Emily watched as he destroyed another male. Seven left plus the one perched in the tree. Chills ran down her spine when Tryton waved at her. She noticed he had the same weapons Ayden did. A loud boom caused her to jump. "Six more." She grabbed another clip and reloaded her pistol. She looked up right away when she heard Ayden grimace in pain. A female demon had embedded her dagger in his shoulder. "No, no." Emily lifted her pistol and fired at the male demon that was approaching Ayden. "Oh damn it," she muttered when the male came straight towards her.

Ayden pulled the dagger from his shoulder and threw it back at the female demon hitting her in the neck.

He glanced up and saw Emily was in trouble. He charged at the male demon knocking him to the ground. "Ahh!!" Ayden cried out when the male sunk his claws into his chest.

"Get off him you bastard!" Emily yelled, emptying her gun into the male demon.

Ayden kicked the male off then quickly chopped his head off, but he was too slow to get up and was thrown back by the blast.

Emily could see Ayden was moving slower and his wounds were slow to heal. "No damn it," she growled, grabbing her last clip. She slammed the clip into the gun and took aim at the next demon. "Four more," she whispered when Ayden finished off the female. But again he didn't clear the blast.

Tryton smiled, watching Ayden grow weaker. "What the fuck?" He noticed Ayden's shoulder wound slowly closing. "Ah, a healer, how interesting, you are part angel…huh."

Two demons attacked Ayden at the same time, cutting him deep. He heard Emily's gun go off and one of the demons grimaced. Ayden kicked one away and quickly sliced the other's throat. He jumped up and kicked the demon's head off. This time he avoided the blast. He felt another demon's claws go into his back. He was getting too many wounds for his body to heal and he was beginning to feel the effects of losing too much blood.

Alma got ready to charge at Ayden again. She licked Ayden's blood from her sword. This time she would kill him. She looked up at Tryton as he stood up on the tree branch.

"Stand down," Tryton said, jumping down from the tree. He walked over to Alma and ran his hand tenderly through her hair. "Very well done." He smiled at her.

"Thank you Tryton," she replied like an eager puppy.

"I will have to reward you when we are finished." He ran his tongue over her lips then headed towards Ayden.

Alma could barely catch her breath as the anticipation filled her body.

Ayden slowly went towards Emily. There was no way he could defeat a demon as strong as Tryton in the condition he was in.

"You will fight me, son of Asurul," Tryton bellowed as he scraped his hand blades together.

Ayden caressed Emily's face then softly kissed her lips. "Emily, I am sorry."

"Don't be." She cupped his face in her hands.

"I can't leave you to those demons."

Emily felt the point of Ayden's blade on her neck. "We will be together in the next life." She kissed him one last time. "I love you Ayden."

"I love you, Emily." He closed his eyes and took her into his arms. He held his hand blade to her throat. He wanted just one more minute, just one. He breathed in the scent of her, enjoyed the warmth of her.

"Come on Ayden," Tryton growled.

Ayden looked into Emily's eyes. There was only love in them. "Close your eyes." She slowly closed her eyes and waited for his blade.

Ayden was startled by the large blast. He grabbed the tree and steadied himself. He quickly turned around and saw Asurul standing before Tryton. "Father!"

Emily looked over Ayden's shoulder at the dark-haired man, his body was strong and lean, he had two hand blades similar to Ayden's out and ready to use. He looked like he was just in a battle, but the hatred that brewed in his dark eyes seemed to give him strength.

"You, what are you doing here? The Creator forbade you to interfere," Tryton growled.

"I will deal with the Creator's anger later. You will not touch my son."

"Nothing will save him and now, finally I can kill you too."

"You can try, but I remember everything about you."

"Shut up and fight!"

"I remember a fledgling who was willing to do anything to gain the knowledge of his superiors."

"Shut up," Tryton growled.

Asurul had to buy Ayden just a little more time to heal. There were still a three of Tryton's peons left alive. "Did you like being Syn's little dog? He made you fetch him anything he wanted. Or Kali, tell me, was it nice being her plaything. Of course Manus…"

"Shut the fuck up!"

"Did you like the taste of his cock? Or perhaps you liked the feel of his whip against your body?"

"You abandon me." Tryton visibly shook from the intensity of his emotions. "You were supposed to finish my training and make me into a true General, but you found that damn angel and she corrupted your soul."

"Isa saved my soul, though I don't expect someone like you to understand. You thought we were what….brothers in arms? I was ordered by Lasax to train you, so I did what I was told to do."

"You didn't torment me like the others, I thought…"

"You thought what, that I actually gave a shit about you? I trained several demons to become Generals, what made you think you were something special? Tormenting my student would have been a waste of my time. Besides, you were so eager to learn from those other three, you did whatever they asked no matter how twisted their request."

"I wanted to impress you!" Tryton was breathing hard as his anger surged through his body.

"You disgust me, just like those other three did."

"You are no different than me, Asurul. No different, do you hear me? Once I kill you I am going to tear your son apart."

"Arrhhhh!!" Asurul yelled as he charged at Tryton.

Asurul was amazing as he easily repelled Tryton's attacks. Tryton's anger drove him on. He had forgotten just how skilled Asurul was. But nothing would stop him from satiating his need for vengeance. Asurul's words cut him worse than he wanted to admit. But he would have to focus. He hissed as Asurul's blade slashed his upper arm.

"No!!!" Alma yelled. She wouldn't let any harm come to Tryton. She charged straight at Asurul.

"Emily stay here." Ayden charged at one of the male demons taking advantage of the distraction his father gave. He wasted no time slicing off his head. He quickly spotted Alma and raced for her. He tackled her just before she reached Asurul. He held her to him and quickly sliced her throat then he grabbed her and threw her from where Asurul was fighting.

"Tryton…" she coughed and sputtered… "I love you, I am sorry I failed you…"

Ayden hurried back towards her and sliced her head off. He leapt in the air to clear the blast. He attacked the last demon, wanting no one to interfere with Asurul's fight, then he collapsed to the ground.

"Ayden!" Emily hurried over to him. She tore strips off her shirt. She carefully wrapped the deepest cuts hoping to buy his body time to heal. When she was finished, she propped him up so he could watch his father battle with Tryton. Asurul moved with such speed and skill that it was beyond words to describe.

Ayden watched his father attack Tryton. He had never seen his father in a real battle before and his skill was most impressive. Even so, Ayden focused on healing just in case Asurul needed him.

"Ayden."

Emily looked up and saw a woman, who could only be described as angelic rush over to them.

"Mother."

Emily looked into Isa's beautiful blue eyes. Never had she seen such compassion or love before, displayed so openly.

"You must be Emily."

"Yes." Emily watched Isa quickly stand up when Asurul cried out.

Tryton's blade had slashed him in the thigh, but Asurul quickly got back up ignoring the pain.

"I have to help him," Ayden said, trying to sit up.

"You are too weak, besides, Tryton can't defeat Asurul." Isa placed her hand on Ayden's worse wound, helping him to heal himself.

"No one will threaten my son again!" Asurul cried out as he sliced off Tryton's head. The blast was so strong it knocked all three of them back.

"Emily." Ayden reached over to her.

"I am okay, don't worry."

"Isa!!" Asurul yelled as he raced over to her and scooped her up into his arms.

"I will be fine." She wrapped her arms around him.

"Why did you come?"

"I wanted to help our son too."

"No, my Isa, I didn't want you to see me as I once was." He nuzzled his cheek against her.

Emily watched the two of them. Their love for each other was undeniable. "An angel and a demon," she whispered, unable to take her eyes off them.

"Emily stay with me and don't say anything." Ayden pulled her into his arms and leaned up against a tree.

Emily felt a strong evil presence. "Oh my God." Her breath caught. A large being emerged from the ground, it had to be more than seven feet tall, it looked like a man, his black hair hung down to its feet, but it looked more like fur. It had cat-like eyes and pointed teeth.

"Lasax," Ayden whispered.

Emily was terrified. This Lasax was the leader of Hell. There was no way Asurul and Ayden could kill him.

"You broke the Creator's rule, Asurul. Now I can kill you," Lasax roared.

Emily felt another presence upon them. She couldn't move when the image of a most beautiful man appeared.

"Prolo," Ayden said as he grabbed Emily's hand tight.

"Lasax, calm down."

Lasax roared at Prolo as he snapped his teeth.

"What the hell now?" Emily looked, feeling yet another strong presence approaching.

"You will not interfere," a quiet voice said.

Emily's eyes widened seeing the shadowy figure appear. This one was hard to make out.

"Necoblas." Ayden felt his strength quickly returning to him, almost as if Necoblas was healing him. Then just as suddenly as Prolo, Lasax and Necoblas appeared, they were gone.

"What happened?" Emily asked.

"I don't know." Ayden came up to his feet and then helped Emily up. He walked over to Isa and Asurul. "What is happening?"

"Asurul will stand trial before the Creator." Isa wept. Ayden watched as Asurul took Isa into his arms.

"What does that mean?"

"It means I might lose my soul for disobeying the Creator."

"No," Ayden growled. "If you knew the price, why did you come down here?"

"You needed me."

"So does mother." Ayden felt Emily's small hand grab his. He squeezed hard. "Let me talk to the Creator." Ayden didn't like that look on his parents face as if they knew something he didn't. "What?" Before they could answer they disappeared.

"I will not let my father's soul be destroyed because of me." Ayden felt a rage build inside him. The Creator wouldn't take his father's soul for just protecting him, would he/she? No, not because of him, everything his parents gave up, endured…because of him.

Emily didn't know what to say or do. She quickly looked up when she heard footsteps approaching them. "Now what?" She was relieved to see Michael and Ryo approaching.

"What has happened?" Ryo asked, scanning the area.

"Are you all right?" Michael asked, looking over Ayden. But Ayden had his eyes fixed up at the sky. Anger brewed in his eyes. Michael slowly backed away from Ayden. He could feel Ayden's rage.

"Creator, you will not take my father's soul!" Ayden shouted to the sky. "Do you hear me!!" Ayden let go of Emily's hand and let his hand blades emerge. "You will not take his soul!!!!" Ayden sliced away at a tree until it fell over.

Michael placed his hand on Emily's shoulder to stop her from going to Ayden. "Let him vent."

Ryo and Michael both just stood there and watched Ayden. Never had they seen such fury come from him. They didn't understand what had happened, or why Asurul was going to lose his soul.

Michael looked down when he felt Emily grab his hand. "What do we do?" she quietly asked.

"Leave him alone and wait for him to tell us what he needs."

Chapter 17

"What's happening?" Gabriele asked as she went to Michael. Miranda, Ryker and Jasmine stood back, per her request. She knew she was supposed to wait for Michael and Ryo to return, but she just couldn't. Tasmos and a couple of his fellow Archangels helped Gabriele bring the others here.

"Asurul was taken to stand trial," Emily answered. She wanted to go to Ayden to try and do something, anything to help him. But he was lashing out, destroying tree after tree. She hated seeing him like this, but hated more that she couldn't do anything to help Asurul for Ayden. Hell, she didn't even know just what had happened.

"Asurul has gone against the Creator, so too has Isa. Finally they will be judged by the Creator," Tasmos added. He had no love for Asurul, and he was still angry at Isa for lowering herself to love a demon. As far as he was concerned they were getting what they deserved.

Ayden turned around and glared back at Tasmos. "You have aided my hunters so I will forgive your words."

Tasmos just looked at Ayden, not saying a word.

"Thank you for helping me again, Tasmos," Gabriele said.

Tasmos nodded his head towards her and took to the sky with the other two Archangels. Prolo had summoned them back.

Gabriele watched him fly away.

"Why did you bring Miranda here?" Michael asked. He wasn't to damn happy that Gabriele brought Miranda when he asked her not to.

"I wanted to help you and Ryo. Besides she insisted that she wanted to come too. I tried my best to convince those three to stay where they were, but they wouldn't hear of it."

"Ryker wanted to protect you didn't he?"

"Of course he did."

"He has put my Miranda in danger."

"Please don't start fighting," Emily injected. "We have to do something to help Ayden."

Emily grabbed a hold of Michael's arm as the earth under her feet shook. Michael held onto her and looked back at Miranda. Ryker had placed his arms in front of Miranda and Jasmine and they held onto him to steady themselves. He looked over at Ryo as he held onto Gabriele. They both just looked at each other; both didn't know what was happening or what they should be doing.

"Emily!" Ayden called as he tried to fight the forces that were pulling him away from this realm.

"Ayden!" Emily raced over to him and reached out her hand to grab his, but in a matter of seconds, he disappeared. . "Where is he?" she spun around and looked at the rest of the group.

"I don't know." Michael felt a strange tickling sensation race through his body as too did Ryo and Gabriele. They too disappeared.

"What the hell is going on?" Ryker gathered up the women and pulled out his pistol.

"Something is really wrong," Jasmine said, looking around. "Ryker!" She pointed up to the sky. Four Archangels swooped down at them.

"Is it Tasmos?" Miranda couldn't tell.

"No it isn't," Jasmine said, watching the four angels coming closer.

"All right, if they attack, we have to grab the silver dagger they carry." Ryker threw down his pistol; it was useless against an Archangel.

The four men landed a few feet in front of them. "Calm down mortals," the largest of the four said.

Ryker noticed they didn't have their weapons drawn. "Where are the hunters and Ayden?"

"They are to witness Asurul's trial."

"Take us to them," Ryker demanded.

"You are mortal and not allowed to witness the trial."

"Take us to them, or I swear by the Creator I will kill you all." Ryker stretched out his arms and motioned for the women to stand back.

The largest angel started to laugh. "I witnessed your battle with the demons, mortal. I told Tasmos he shouldn't aid you."

"Then why did he?"

"He owed the huntress Gabriele a debt. You really mean to challenge all four of us don't you mortal male?"

"If need be."

"Please, if there is anyway for us to witness Asurul's trial…" Emily moved forward. "Asurul is Ayden's father; I can't let Ayden go through this alone. I beg of you to take us to them."

Ryker quickly grabbed Emily and placed her back behind him.

Suddenly all four Archangels fell to one knee and bowed their heads. Emily held her breath as Prolo appeared before them.

"You are most amusing Ryker," Prolo laughed.

Ryker remembered his stay in Heaven and the cruelty Prolo dished out. But even this would not sway him.

He had to get to Gabriele and he knew the women he protected felt the same way about their soul mates.

Ryker tried to grab Emily as she made her way to Prolo. She came down to her knees in front of Prolo and bowed her head. "Please take me to Ayden and allow the others to be with their soul mates."

"Why should I allow this?"

"You are the leader of Heaven." Emily slowly looked up into his beautiful face. "I always believed that Heaven was a place of great love and mercy. Looking upon you I see a light about you that Lasax doesn't have. I believe in my heart, you of all the great ones must be capable of mercy and compassion. So please take me to Ayden, he needs me."

Prolo regarded her for a moment. "Would you be willing to give anything to be by Ayden's side?"

"Yes."

"Even your soul?"

"Yes."

Prolo looked down at Emily. Her love for Ayden was absolute, and he believed she would give anything to be able to ease Ayden's pain. "All right, I will allow you mortals to witness Asurul's trial. But you will not be able to stand with Ayden or his hunters. However they will know you are there."

Emily reached up for his hand and gently kissed it. "Thank you great Prolo."

Prolo helped her to her feet then turned to his Archangels. "Take them to the trial." With that Prolo disappeared. He had planned to have the mortals taken somewhere safe while the trial was going on. He wasn't planning on coming himself, but Ryker was giving his angels a hard time and the mortals had to be moved quickly. Lasax was already plotting to kill all of them while the hunters and Ayden was busy with the trial. Prolo believed this act would have been pity and pointless. Besides, he loved to piss Lasax off. Honoring Emily's request accomplished this and having them there would irritate Lasax to no end.

"Emily…" Ryker didn't know what to say, but he was grateful for what she had done. He may not be able to hold Gabriele, but at least she would know he was there.

"I suggest you hold on," the large Archangel said as he lifted Ryker over his shoulder and took flight. Ryker looked behind them and saw the others were following.

෮෮෮

Ayden stood with his three hunters beside him. They were in a large arena. Off to the right Lasax sat with several of his demons next to him. Off to the left sat Prolo with several of his Archangels beside him. Ayden looked right across from where he and his hunters were and saw Necoblas sitting alone.

"Ayden," Gabriele gasped, seeing Asurul brought into the middle of the arena in chains.

Ayden looked down and saw Isa was standing against the wall with one arm chained to it. Isa smiled up to Ayden trying to reassure him, but he could feel her fear for Asurul.

"What did Isa do?" Ryo grabbed the stone railing that was in front of them. He couldn't stand here and watch her get harmed. Seeing her chained like some animal was bad enough. Isa was the kindest, gentlest, person he had ever known. She was almost like a mother to him. He would not stand for her being treated this way. But what could he really do to stop it?

"She came down to help my father," Ayden replied. He was powerless to help his parents. After the hundreds of years they watched over him, he couldn't do a damn thing to aid them.

"Ryker?" Gabriele latched onto the stone railing. Ryker, Jasmine, Miranda and Emily were seated close to Necoblas. "Oh no, they aren't ….dead are they?" Her heart slammed into her chest.

"No, Gabriele they are not dead." Ayden squeezed her hand. He watched Emily come up to her feet and point up to where he was. He wanted so much to reach out and touch her, but the stone railing prevented him from going to her. He was trapped in this area. He saw the distressed look in Emily's eyes as she looked down at Isa and Asurul.

"Ayden, I am here, whatever happens I am here," her sweet voice flooded his mind bringing him a measure of calm.

"Emily I hear you."

"Ayden, I love you."

"You have no idea what hearing you say those words means to me."

"She begged Prolo to bring them here," Gabriele said, holding onto Ayden's hand. "Ryker told me what she had done."

Ayden looked at his hunters. He could see they too were calmer with their soul mates here. Ayden then looked over to Prolo and bowed his head to him, gesturing a thank you to him.

"Ayden what is coming?"

"The Creator, Emily, he/she will appear as you perceive the Creator to be."

Some saw the Creator as male, others saw a female. Ayden however saw both and at first it was distracting, but soon he adjusted.

"I see we are all here." The Creator's voice was neither male nor female, but a mixture of both. "Asurul I commanded you to stay in your paradise with Isa, and yet you disobeyed me. You were not allowed to meddle in fate."

"My son needed me; surely you can't fault me for wanting to protect my child," Asurul growled as he struggle with his chains. "Isa has done nothing, why must she be chained?"

"Ayden is no longer a child. You disobeyed me."

"What did Isa do?"

"She escaped your paradise to aid you. She too was forbidden to leave."

"You can't do this to her, she doesn't deserve this." Asurul stop struggling with his chains, it was pointless.

"Isa's soul is pure, from the moment of conception through her mortal life, her heart remained pure."

Ayden was taken back when flashes of Isa's life filled his mind. She lived in early times and struggled to make her village a good place. She gave everything she had to help the people of her village.

The arena filled with these images. Asurul watched the countless selfless acts Isa preformed as a mortal and a guardian angel. Asurul saw Isa's mortal life, the brief time she was married before her husband died of a disease. The child she miscarried. She never married again after that. He watched the countless deeds she had done as a guardian angel, bringing calm to the souls she protected over the years.

Ayden watched everything. The kindness, the selflessness of his mother and the love she gave so freely to everyone around her. "Then why is she chained like an animal now?" Ayden couldn't stop the words that sprung from his mouth.

"Be careful Ayden, for you had yet to see your father as he was."

"Ayden, please my son, don't speak," Isa shouted to him.

"Unchain my mother!" Ayden yelled as he pounded on the railing, a shock knocked him backwards and Ryo helped him back to his feet.

"Ayden, you must remain calm," Ryo said as he looked up at the Creator. To him the Creator had taken the form of a woman.

"Ayden, I know it pains you to see your mother like this, but please do as she says." Emily tried to calm him.

Ayden could feel Emily's distress. He decided not to say anymore for now. He continued to watch his mother's life play out. He gasped seeing her standing in front of a small child prepared to give up her life to protect the child from the oncoming lesser-demons. Through her eyes he saw his father. The shock Isa felt when a demon General saved her from the lesser-demons. The lustful thoughts that filled her mind when she saw Asurul again.

Ayden tried to look away but was unable to. He felt her lust quickly turn to love and her resolve to give up everything to stand by Asurul's side. Then everything she went through just to be with Asurul. Their mortal lives they shared with each other was a brief period of bliss. He felt the love his mother had for him and the joy she felt holding him as a baby in her arms. Then he felt her angst at watching him suffer over and over through all of this.

"NOOO!!!!" Asurul screamed. He couldn't take seeing Isa's pain or having Ayden witnessing it.

"She suffered because of you," Prolo spoke up, "you filthy demon."

"I say that he livened up her boring life," Lasax chuckled.

"Silence," the Creator commanded.

"Noooo," Asurul sobbed. "Isa, I am sorry."

"Asurul, you don't apologize, you hear me. You showed me love."

"I showed you misery." He didn't deserve her love and yet, she gives it freely and completely. His heart felt like it was being torn in two. "I don't deserve you, Isa," he quietly said.

"Stop this!" Ayden cried out. Asurul's pain raked through him. "Why put them through this?"

"You will see Ayden."

The images changed. A battlefield in early medieval times filled the arena. Countless men died before them. Ayden gasped seeing Asurul in bloody armor running his sword through an unarmed man. He watched as Asurul moved through the battlefield killing any of his enemy that still lived. No mercy, no remorse, only a thirst, a need for vengeance and death.

"Isa and Ayden don't look!" Asurul cried. "Please don't see me as I was."

"All must see you for what you were." The Creator forced Isa and Ayden to watch, multiplying Asurul's pain and shame.

"Are you afraid to see yourself demon?" Prolo asked.

"A Grand General is what I see, Prolo," Lasax added.

Ayden could barely watch as he saw his father go from battle to battle. Killing, destroying everyone he perceived as an enemy. Ayden felt like the wind was knocked out of him when he saw his father as a boy. Alone, neglected, mistreated by the very people who were supposed to love him. His mother treated him as though he was a disease, and his father only wanted someone like him, a killer.

Michael gasped seeing himself in the small Asurul. He too never knew his mother's love and was only trained to become a killing machine.

"Asurul saw himself in you Michael." Isa's voice filled Michael's mind as she felt the intensity of his emotions.

Ayden looked over at Michael. The understanding and pity in Michael's face told him Michael knew what Asurul had lived through as a child. He also felt Michael's own shame at the countless lives he took as a paid killer.

"Don't do this to yourself Michael." Miranda's voice brought calm to Michael.

"Stop this!" Asurul cried. "Why must I relive my mortal life? Why must my family witness this?"

"It is necessary, Asurul." The Creator raised a hand a clear signal for Asurul to be silent.

Isa slid down the wall as she cried for Asurul. "Why make him relive this, Creator?" Isa cried.

"Silence!"

"Michael, be calm." Ayden touched Michael's shoulder and within moments calm spread through Michael's body.

Ayden watched his mother struggle with the chain that held her arm to the wall. His attention was forced back to the images of his father committing one atrocious act after another.

Then blackness filled the arena. Ayden saw Lasax pulling Asurul's soul from the depths of Purgatory and how easily Asurul adjusted to being a General of Hell. He watched his father train other demons. He saw the hatred Asurul had for Syn, seeing him as a rival for Lasax's attention. He felt the admiration Asurul had for Lasax.

"Ayden forgive me," Asurul quietly said as he looked up at his son. That look of disbelief on Ayden's face broke his heart. He wouldn't blame his son if he hated him now. But please don't let him say it out loud. Hearing his son say he hated him would tear him apart.

Ayden watched as Asurul emerged on earth, then as though someone just slammed on the brakes, Ayden was thrust forward. The conflicting emotions that boiled within Asurul as he laid eyes on Isa filled Ayden.

"What are you doing to him?" Asurul struggled with his chains as he watched Ayden leaning over the stone rails almost as if he was going to be sick.

Ayden saw through Asurul's eyes as he watched Isa try to defend the child. The anger Asurul had at Prolo for not helping one of his own kind. Then the spark of humanity that ignited in Asurul's soul as he leapt down and saved Isa from the lesser-demons. Ayden felt his father's lust for his mother and conflicting emotions that raged inside him. Compassion and mercy were born in Asurul's soul as he fought with his lust and need to please Lasax. He didn't want Isa to corrupt her soul. Love blossomed from the moment Isa touched him.

"Father!!!" Ayden yelled as he felt everything Asurul did.

"Stop tormenting my son!" Asurul fought harder with his restraints.

Tears came to Ayden's eyes as he felt his father's love for him. The moment his father laid eyes on him, he loved him. Ayden was the combined soul of Isa and Asurul, and Ayden felt ever ounce of love his father had for him. The protectiveness, the resolve his father had that nothing of Heaven, Hell, Purgatory or Earth would ever hurt the little boy who was part of him and Isa. Ayden started to cry when he felt Asurul's guilt of not being able to show his love for his son or his beloved Isa. And the overwhelming despair Asurul felt that his words condemned Ayden to suffer.

He watched his father slam into the barrier that held him in his paradise, preventing him from helping. Ayden felt the pain rack through him as he felt every cut, every bruise his father endured trying to get to him. He felt his father's resolve to stop Tryton from destroying his son, the sheer determination to get to him in time, the angst as he watched Tryton closing in. Asurul would let nothing stop him from protecting his son, not even losing his soul. Ayden felt every emotion Asurul had.

"You disobeyed me Asurul." The Creator stopped the images.

"He was trying to protect me!" Ayden wailed. "Both of them protected me through my whole existence. Allow me to do the same for them. Take my soul if you must have some sort of payment."

"No!!" Asurul and Isa shouted together.

"Regardless of your emotions, Ayden, he disobeyed my command. Tell me Asurul, if I granted you the chance to obey me and let fate play out…would you?"

"I saved my son's soul." Asurul looked up at the Creator. "I would do nothing different."

"Then you give me no choice but…"

"No!" Isa slipped her bloody hand from the cuff and hurried over to Asurul. "If you take his soul you must take mine as well."

"Isa, go back."

"My place is with you."

"Isa please allow me to give you back your soul."

"Creator, if you take Asurul's soul, you must take mine. For I am the other half of his soul and I can't survive without him." Isa wrapped her arms around Asurul's neck and held him tightly.

Everything fell silent.

"Ayden reach out to me, take comfort from my soul"

"Emily…" Ayden's soul reached for hers and he felt her love for him.

The Creator lifted a hand signaling Asurul and Isa to rise up to their feet. "Asurul you have earned redemption."

Asurul was freed from his chains. He wrapped his arms around Isa and held her tightly.

"But didn't he already earn redemption when you forbade me from killing him?" Lasax asked.

"No, he was simply granted the chance to earn redemption."

"You gave those two a paradise," Prolo added.

"Asurul could have stayed within his paradise, but his love for his son would not allow it."

"He disobeyed you," Lasax growled.

"He truly risked his soul, he knew it and yet he was willing to give up his soul to protect his son and to spare Isa the pain of losing her son. This selfless act from a man who cared little for anyone or anything, this selfless act from a man who knew little about love until he was shown love, this selfless act from a man who once enjoyed killing his enemies. Asurul has earned his redemption."

"Ayden." Emily wept as she watched the tears roll down his face. She looked down at Asurul and Isa, never had she seen two people love each other this intensely, completely before.

"I will give you this kind of love Emily."

"Ayden…" Emily felt Ryker's arm go around her as she cried openly.

"Beautiful isn't it?" Ryker wiped the tears from Emily's face.

"Beyond beauty," was all she could reply.

"Ayden, now is the time you must choose what fate has decreed for you and what your heart wants," the Creator's voice rung out.

"Leave my son alone," Asurul growled.

"Father you have done enough for me. Enjoy your paradise with mother, for you have earned it." Ayden stood tall before the Creator and waited to hear what his fate was.

Asurul looked up at his son, pride and love filled him. "He is so much like you, Isa." He held her tighter.

"No, he is the best of both of us."

"Necoblas' soul has grown weary." The Creator took the form of a woman. "You, Ayden have been chosen to take his place as the ruler of Purgatory."

"Me..." Ayden paused for a moment. "I am not worthy to be the leader of Purgatory.

"You are worthy," Necoblas spoke up.

"However, you must choose."

"Choose...I don't understand."

"You must choose between your fate and Emily."

"What?" Ayden looked over at Emily. "How can you ask me to choose? I waited for her for so many years and now that I have found the other half of my soul, I have to give her up to do what I was born to do. That is why I was born, wasn't it? You planned for me to take Necoblas' place all along."

"I was hopeful you could be the one to let Necoblas rest and you have proven yourself worthy. Your compassion, love and gentle nature will restore Purgatory to what it once was."

The Creator waved a hand and twenty men entered the arena.

"Saban," Ryo said as he watched Saban enter the arena.

"Who are these men?" Gabriele asked.

"Demon hunters." Michael recognized a couple of the men.

"These men gave their lives and put their souls in limbo, for you Ayden. Each one of these men knew you were meant for something great. Each one willingly put everything on the line for you. They believed in you, Ayden."

Emily looked out over the arena and spotted Saban he was standing beside several other men. All of them appeared to be in a dazed state. "What is going on?"

"I don't know," Ryker replied.

Ayden's heart broke looking at all his hunters. He remembered each one of them. But his eyes locked on Saban. He was willing to wait to be with his soul mate Geneva. He willingly gave his life to protect his fellow hunters' soul mates.

"How can I choose?" Ayden quietly said. "Will all of their souls be lifted from limbo?"

"You would have the power to do this for them."

Ayden felt a strange pulling feeling, then he found himself down in the arena with Emily standing beside him.

"Ayden." Emily wrapped her arms around him. "What is going on?"

"I am to be the next ruler of Purgatory."

Emily looked into his beautiful golden eyes. "When, how?"

"If I accept I will not be able to be with you."

Emily reached up her hand and stroked his cheek, then let her fingers run through his golden hair. "We will be together again. If you are to be the leader of Purgatory, when I die, I will see you again."

Ayden pulled her closer to him and kissed her deeply. Her words touched him profoundly. "I don't want to let you go," he whispered against her lips.

"We will be together again." Emily tried to stop her tears. But she couldn't stop him from becoming what he was meant to be. She couldn't stand to see the despair in his eyes. He had said his hunters were like family. She knew he couldn't leave them like this.

"Choose Ayden."

Ayden cupped Emily's face in his hands. "I love you Emily." He kissed her one last time.

"I love you Ayden." Emily fought back her tears. She would not let him see her cry.

"I am ready to be what I was born to be." He watched Emily slowly disappear. His heart ached, but he held himself together. He looked up to Gabriele, Michael and Ryo. "Thank you for everything you have done for me." He turned to Ryker, Miranda and Jasmine. "Take good care of my hunters."

"Ayden." Isa and Asurul went to him.

"You let Emily go," Asurul placed his hand on Ayden's back. He could feel his son's pain and it tore at him. Ayden was a greater man than Asurul could ever hope to be.

"I will see her again." Ayden watched his parents fade away, followed by the others. He was alone now.

"Thank you, though the words seem insufficient to express my gratitude," Necoblas said as he to begun to fade away.

"You must be strong now, Ayden." The Creator waved a hand and Ayden found himself in Purgatory.

"So many," he said, looking out across the sea of souls. He felt strange, and soon everything he needed to know filled his mind. His body surged with a strange power. He focused his mind and found Saban. Within moments Saban was by his side.

"Ayden?" Saban looked around. Ayden could tell Saban was afraid. Ayden closed his eyes and Saban was back in that quaint little house he shared with Geneva.

"Geneva!" Saban called out.

"Saban!" She ran into the house and jumped into his arms.

Ayden watched their beautiful reunion. They waited long enough to be together again. Ayden left them alone.

He began painting Purgatory by using the memories of all the souls that resided here. He closed his eyes and pictured the forest where he and Emily made love. His heart already ached for her.

"We will be together again, Emily," Ayden whispered. She was the other half of him. After centuries of searching, he found his soul mate. He had to believe they would be together again. They were meant to be and he was willing to wait forever for her.

He went back to work waking all his old hunters making their transition easy. Saban and Geneva were granted their own paradise. He asked this of the Creator. His other hunters either became Archangels or their souls were reborn, either way they were no longer in limbo.

Ayden grew tired and he headed back to the copy of the forest that he and Emily had shared so much. He lay in the grass and went to sleep.

Necoblas looked at Ayden sleeping, then he looked out over Purgatory. Slowly the grayness was being replaced by a warm glow. He watched as souls, who lumbered in limbo, slowly awoke. Ayden's warmth was slowly blanketing Purgatory, returning it to the place Necoblas remembered.

"Creator, I am ready." Necoblas looked down at Ayden. "This is how I started, until the loneliness grew to be too much." Necoblas felt his outer shell melting away. Soon his soul would be reborn. The Creator blessed him with a second chance.

Chapter 18

Emily walked into the hospital with two large bouquets of flowers in her hands. She needed to see Shelly and Diane. She wanted to make sure they were okay, but more so just to be around her old friends. Emily's heart was breaking. It was one thing to have Scott divorce her, she could deal with that. But to lose the man of her dreams because he was the leader of Purgatory now, well her mind was having trouble dealing with it. In fact her whole ordeal was enough to send anyone to the nuthouse. Sometimes she would wonder if Ayden was even real, did she make up the whole thing. However, she knew in her heart he was real and this made her arms ache to hold him.

"Hey, Emily." Shelly smiled.

"How are you guys?" Emily handed each one flowers.

"We are getting better. It's damn lucky we got out of the house," Diane said as she smelt the roses.

"Out of the house?" Emily sat down on the bed. She thought Ayden had cleared their memories.

"Apparently there was a carbon monoxide leak in our house. Lucky for us the cable guy was schedule to show up that day or me and Diane would have been dead. Scary when you think about it. I thought you knew this already."

"Oh you should have seen that cable guy too. Wow was he gorgeous; of course I was half drugged from the carbon monoxide at the time."

"What did he look like?"

"Tall, blond, gorgeous and oh, did he have a yummy body," Shelly interjected.

"What about his eyes?"

"His eyes, I was to busy looking at the rest of him." Shelly chuckled.

"They were a beautiful golden color. I never seen anybody with eyes that color before that is why it sticks out in my mind," Diane added.

"Golden eyes…" Emily began to cry.

"Hey, what's wrong?" Shelly scooted down the bed and wrapped her arms around Emily.

"It's been a long week." Emily quickly pulled herself together. "I am glad you two are feeling better."

"Don't worry about that stupid Scott. You will find someone so much better," Shelly said as she hugged Emily tighter.

Emily broke down and cried her eyes out. She did find someone else much better. Ayden was a dream, a beautiful wonderful dream.

"Emily…" Diane walked over to the bed and hugged Emily too. "Screw Scott, when I get back on my feet I am going to hunt him down like the dirty dog he is."

Emily let her tears fall. She couldn't tell her friends why she was crying but it felt good just to let it all go.

ഈഈഈ

Gabriele looked at the address Ryker dug up for her. It was strange being just a normal woman again. Her hunter skills slowly began fading away once Ayden became the ruler of Purgatory. Ryker however was thrilled when the last of her hunter skills faded. One, she wouldn't be in danger anymore. Lasax and Prolo were forbidden to harm any of them. And two, he was finally able to beat her in a play fight. Gabriele couldn't help but chuckle. Ryker certainly loved being the alpha male.

Gabriele walked up the steps of the little house and rang the doorbell. She smiled when Emily answered the door. "Hello, may I come in?"

"Of course." Emily showed her into Shelly and Diane's house. Emily was helping the two get back on their feet, so she moved in with them for a little while.

"How are your friends?" Gabriele sat down on the sofa and took the cup of coffee Emily offered. "It feels nice to actually want to eat and drink again." She took a sip of her coffee and savored the flavor.

"You are no longer a hunter?" Emily sat down on the chair across from her.

"No, there is no longer a need for demon hunters."

"What brings you by?"

Gabriele sat her coffee down on the table. "I wanted to check up on you for Ayden."

"You can still talk to him?" Emily started to get excited.

"No, but for some reason Michael can. So Ayden wanted him to check up on you, and since me and Ryker are close by, I told Michael I would do it. Miranda is pregnant and Michael is slipping into his role of overprotective father early."

"Miranda is pregnant, oh how wonderful for them. What about Ryo and Jasmine?"

"They moved to Japan. Jasmine wanted to see where Ryo lived when he was mortal. Of course a lot has changed since then, but he honored her request. She wants to have a family soon, too."

"What about you?"

"Oh, I can wait for children. I don't think Ryker is ready to have another child yet. Besides, Ryker is going out on a mission soon and I am coming with him."

"Mission?"

"He is going back to the Special Forces Unit. He wanted to account for the men he lost when Kali attacked them. Of course Ryker had to make something up, who would believe him if he said a demon bitch slaughtered his whole unit. They assumed Ryker had suffered from traumatic stress or something to that affect. It was important to Ryker to let the families of his men know what had happened to them. Besides, Ryker isn't the nine to five, suburban husband type, and I think I will like going out into the field with him. After being a hunter for so long I don't think I could handle a regular life either. Making identification for me, Michael and Ryo was quite simple. Jasmine helped us in this department. Since she had been on the run from her husband for so long it was rather easy for her to create a fake past for us three hunters. "

"I am glad to hear everyone is doing well." Emily paused for a moment. "How is Ayden?"

"Here." Gabriele reached into her jacket pocket and pulled out a letter. "I will just go into the kitchen and let you enjoy your letter in private." Gabriele handed Emily the letter then left the room.

Emily's hands shook as she began reading the letter

My Dearest Emily,

I am able to still speak with Michael, why this is so, I don't know. Perhaps it is his close connection with Asurul, all I know is I am grateful for it. I am so lonely without you beside me. I wait eagerly for the day when I will feel you in my arms again. But until then I don't want you to be unhappy. Live your life to the fullest, Emily. I will be waiting here for you. Know that I love you with all my heart and I feel you in my soul.

Forever yours,
Ayden

Emily held the letter to her breasts and begun to cry.

"It's all right," Gabriele said, placing her hand on Emily's shoulder.

"Do you realize how long I will have to wait to see him again?"

"But the important thing is that you will see Ayden again." Gabriele could feel Emily's pain and she knew Ayden was in pain too. This didn't seem fair. "I know, why don't you come with me. I am sure Ryker would love to see you again."

"Thank you for the offer, but I have to help Shelly and Diane."

"Here." Gabriele reached into her pocket and grabbed a pen. She picked up a piece of paper off the table and scribbled down something then handed it to Emily.

"What is this?"

"This is Michael's phone number and address. When your friends are better why don't you give him a call. And this is mine and Ryker's number and address. You are not alone Emily, you remember that, okay?"

"Thank you." Emily stood up and hugged Gabriele.

Shelly and Diane insisted that Emily go with Gabriele. Emily enjoyed her day with Gabriele and Ryker, being with them some how made her feel connected to Ayden in a strange way.

Emily found the courage to tell Diane and Shelly about Ayden. She suspected they might think her mad, but they didn't. They made her promise to get a hold of Michael. If he could still talk to Ayden, then that was her way to stay in contact with him. Emily did get a hold of Michael once Shelly and Diane were back to themselves.

Chapter 19

Seven months later…

"I can't believe this is taking so long." Michael paced back and forth in the hospital waiting room.

"This is Miranda's first child." Emily tried for the last hour to comfort Michael. The doctor made him leave for a while. Every time Miranda had a contraction Michael would get angrier at the doctor. Oh, he knew it wasn't the doctor's fault but he couldn't stand to see Miranda in so much pain.

"You can come back in if you behave yourself," the nurse said. "Why don't you come in with him?" she said to Emily.

"Would you like me to?" Emily asked Michael.

"Sure, I can yell at you."

Emily chuckled and followed Michael into the delivery room after they got their hospital garb on. Emily went to one side of Miranda while Michael went to the other. Over these last few months Emily had moved next to them, Miranda insisted. After all, Michael could talk with Ayden and Emily needed some way to stay in contact with him. Emily hesitated at first but then accepted their offer. Shelly and Diane were back to their old selves. Emily flew out a couple of times to visit with them and make sure they were getting back on their feet.

"Oh damn it!" Michael growled, holding onto Miranda's hand. "How much longer?"

"Here it comes," the doctor said.

Soon a baby's cry rang out through the room. "It's a boy," the doctor exclaimed, handing Miranda the baby.

Emily watched the joy in Michael's eyes as he gazed into his son's face.

"He is so beautiful," Emily said, looking at the baby.

The nurse took the baby and cleaned it up, then handed him to Michael. "My son, Miranda, our son." He kissed her softly.

"What are you going to name him?" Emily asked.

Miranda looked at Michael. "Well what are we going to name him? You were so sure it was going to be a girl after all."

Michael couldn't take his eyes off his son. "Ayden, I want to name him Ayden."

Emily choked back her tears as Michael handed Miranda the baby. "Ayden, that's your name kiddo." Miranda gently stroked his little cheeks.

"I got to go get me some coffee." Emily excused herself and quickly made a fast exit. She didn't want her sorrow to interfere with their happy moment. Ayden was a perfect name for Michael's son.

Emily sat down and drank her coffee and tried to gather herself. It had been a long seven months. Gabriele, Ryker, Miranda and Michael helped so much, but her heart still felt empty. She took out her sketchpad and turned to her portrait of Ayden. He was lying in that forest opening they made love in. She remembered every detail of his beautiful face and body. She lovingly runs her fingers over his face. "I hope Michael told you his happy news, Ayden," she whispered. "I can almost see you smiling when Michael tells you he named his son after you."

She slowly looked through her sketchpad. She smiled at the picture of Ryker in his army uniform. She turned the page; she had drawn Gabriele in a beautiful dress, a special request from Ryker. She turned the page; there was her portrait of Michael looking out the window of his and Miranda's home. She often found him like this as if he was in his own little world, perhaps he was dealing with his sins of the past, whatever it was he looked to be deep in thought. She turned the page; she had drawn Miranda with her big pregnant belly. Miranda seemed so at peace now. She turned the page to her portrait of Ryo. He was sitting on a tree stump with his long ebony hair dancing in the wind. Jasmine requested this portrait of Ryo. It was an image she had of Ryo from the first time she saw him. She turned to the portrait of Jasmine sitting in a field of flowers, she being the most beautiful flower in the field. This was a request from Ryo. But most of her pictures were of Ayden. The last sketch was one of Asurul and Isa, that moment when the Creator freed Asurul and he held Isa in his arms. She tried to capture the beauty of that moment. She put the sketchpad back in her tote bag.

Emily took a deep breath and headed back to Miranda's room. Michael was holding little Ayden again and poor Miranda looked so tired.

"Feeling better?" Miranda asked.

"Oh yeah that coffee hit the spot." Emily sat down on the chair beside Miranda.

"I am sorry, I should have asked you if naming him Ayden would have upset you," Michael said.

"Oh no, it don't upset me at all. Did you tell Ayden?"

"Yes, he was thrilled for us."

Emily felt a pain in her right arm that was growing worse. It was getting harder to breathe.

"Are you all right?" Miranda asked.

"To much excitement I think."

"Michael, I don't think the doctor has ever encountered someone like you. It wasn't his fault that childbirth hurts." Miranda chuckled.

Emily's chest felt like a heavy weight was sitting on it.

"Emily you don't look so good." Michael handed little Ayden to Miranda and went to her.

The pain in Emily's chest grew worse and worse. Michael ran out of the room and called for a doctor.

"Emily…" Miranda's voice was beginning to fade and everything turned dark.

Michael ran back into the room with a doctor. Emily was lying on the ground. They quickly put her in bed and began working on her.

"Michael, is she all right? What happened, she was just fine yesterday?" Miranda thought it was odd that Michael was smiling. "What are you smiling about?"

"She is going to be with Ayden, soon."

ഏഏഏ

"Emily."

Emily opened her eyes. She slowly sat up. She felt the grass under her hands and saw that she was surrounded by trees. She felt disorientated but yet strangely not afraid.

"Emily."

"Ayden." She quickly looked around and saw him coming closer. He moved strange, almost as if he was part of a dream. "Where am I?"

"Shh, you will be alright in a little while."

"Am I dreaming?"

"No, Emily, you are here with me."

"Here?"

"Purgatory." Ayden's voice kept fading out and her head kept spinning. She felt Ayden's familiar touch and she leaned back into his embrace.

"I am dead?"

"Only your mortal body, Emily."

His scent washed over her, she relished the warmth of his arms. But she had to be dreaming. The last thing she remembered was Miranda having a baby.

"Close your eyes Emily and rest. You will feel no fear."

Emily slowly closed her eyes and fell asleep. Ayden caressed her cheek. Michael had told him what happen and he waited for Emily's soul to make the journey. She was too young to have had a heart attack, but Isa explained to him that Emily had died of a broken heart, just as Asurul had done all those years ago when Isa died. Emily waited for her friends to recover before her body gave out.

Ayden heard the call of souls ready to be reborn and he was compelled to aid them. He gently laid Emily down and covered her with a silken sheet.

After awhile Emily woke up. Everything was clearer now. She remembered this forest where she and Ayden had made love. "Ayden," she called out.

"You are awake." Ayden walked into the clearing.

"Ayden...." Emily couldn't stop her tears; he was really here with her.

Ayden rushed to her and took her into his arms. "Please don't cry." He wiped away the fallen tears and as before, the tears turned into sparkles of light.

"You are really here with me." She ran her hands over his body.

"I will be here with you forever." He pulled her to him and kissed her deeply. "Never again will I let anyone take you from me." He kissed all over her face then lifted her up. With a wave of his hand, a large bed surrounded with flowers appeared. A beautiful waterfall served as a backdrop.

"Oh my…" Emily's breath was taken away.

"You better get use to it, for I have an eternity of love to give you." He removed their clothes with just a thought. He gently lowered her down onto the bed and climbed on top of her.

"Don't make me wait to feel you inside me." Emily wrapped her legs around him and drew him closer. He filled her with one thrust and kept his cock buried to the hilt in her as he took his time kissing her. Slowly he thrust as they intertwined their fingers, both not wanting to let go of the other.

"Emily…" He couldn't find the words to express what he felt at this moment, so he let his body tell her what he felt. He gripped her hand tighter as he thrust faster, kissing her intensely. He could feel her pleasure as she could feel his. It was the most incredible feeling he had ever experienced. He arched up as he felt her orgasm fill her body.

"Ayden look at me," she whispered when she felt his orgasm build. She looked deeply into his golden eyes and watched his pleasure flood him. She felt every delicious moment of his orgasm. The sheer ecstasy of their combine orgasm was nirvana.

He rolled off her and pulled her to him. She snuggled up against him. Her body still tingled from the aftermath of their shared orgasms.

"Whoa…" she exclaimed as she looked up into his beautiful face.

"Whoa is right." He smiled.

"Tell me I am not dreaming, tell me when I awake you will still be here." She wrapped her arm over his chest and held him tightly.

"You are not dreaming and every time you awake I will be right here." He kissed the top of her head.

"What do we do now? I mean you are the ruler of Purgatory, don't you have really important things to do?"

"Yes, I guide souls to their next destination."

"Then what do I do?"

"You comfort my soul. I can make this world anything you want, all you have to do is ask and I will make it so."

"But, I want to help you. I mean there are a lot of souls to guide…"

Ayden placed his fingertips on her lips. "Having you here by my side is everything I need?"

"There is one thing I have been very curious about."

"Oh, what's that?"

Emily slowly kissed down his body until her mouth hovered over his cock. "From the moment you should me your beautiful cock in my dreams, I have been dying to find out what you taste like." She ran her tongue up the length of him.

Ayden watched as she slowly took his cock into her mouth. "Emily," he sighed as his hands tangled in her hair. Her mouth caressed his cock.

"Yum, yum," she cooed as she flicked her tongue over the head of his cock. She could feel the pleasure she was giving him. She loved the sound of his soft moaning and oh that look on his face as he watched her suck on him.

"I am going to cum," he whispered, barely able to get the words out.

"I know, cum in my mouth Ayden."

He grabbed handfuls of her hair as his orgasm started to build and build and build until…"EMILY!!!!" he cried out.

Emily licked the head of his cock one more time, not wanting to waste one drop of his cum. She scooted back up and snuggled in his arms. "Damn you tasted delicious."

"Help yourself anytime you want." He smiled down at her.

"Emily, I can take you anywhere you want to go. Just tell me and I will make it happen."

"Right here in your arms is the only place I want to be for now."

Ayden snuggled her closer and simply enjoyed the feeling of her in his arms. They had all of eternity to enjoy each other. He closed his eyes and let the warmth and love he felt lying here with her fill all of Purgatory.

Epilogue:

Isa looked out over her paradise as a few tears rolled down her face. She felt Asurul's arms wrap around her and she fell back into his embrace.

"What's wrong?" he asked kissing her softly on her neck.

"Emily is with Ayden now. He is so happy." Isa reached up and ran her fingers through Asurul's hair as he continued running soft kisses along her neck. "Our son is safe, he is finally safe."

"Yes, and he has found love, true, real love. Then why are you crying?"

"Joy, sweet, sweet, joy." Isa turned around and looked into Asurul's dark eyes. "This is our paradise." She grabbed his hand and led him out onto the balcony. She pointed off to the east. "Follow me."

Asurul found himself in a small cave. He immediately recognized the cave. "Isa..."

"Do you remember this place?"

"How could I not, this is where we made love for the first time."

"Yes, but this is where I knew I loved you. I want this place to stay in our paradise Asurul."

"But Isa I ...."

"We have buried your past Asurul. But I want this place to stay." Isa looked around. "This small dank little cave changed everything for me. I found the other half of my soul and I knew it here."

"Then I will make sure it stays here. I will love you for eternity Isa. Never will I see pain in those beautiful eyes again. Because of your love, my soul earned redemption, something I thought would never happen."

"But it has Asurul. So no more pain or regret." Isa moved to the opening of the cave. Their paradise seemed endless and it was. "So much to explore I don't even no where to begin."

"I do." Asurul lifted Isa into his arms and carried her back into the cave. He gently sat her down then removed his shirt and laid it on the ground. He scooped her up and then laid her down. "The first time I made love to you here I wrestled with my conscience." He lay down on her, and with a thought, their clothes were gone. He felt Isa's legs wrap around him as his cock entered her. "I know your love, now I want to show you mine."

They unhurriedly made love in that cave. Asurul lay cradled in Isa's arms. For the first time in his existence he felt true peace.

The End

Protector of My Heart Sample chapter

Robin sighed looking out the kitchen window as she mindlessly washed the dishes. Life wasn't living up to her dreams. A nowhere job, no children and a husband who was as romantic as a stick. Charles, her husband was a practical man, wasting money or time on frivolous romantic gestures was beyond him.

Robin closed her eyes, her body stiffened to Charles' touch. "What's wrong did I scare you?" He laughed.

"Yeah." She placed the last dish into the strainer.

"Come on baby, let's go in the bedroom." He rubbed his hard cock against her back. "Got something for you."

Robin knew it was useless to say no. He would pick at her until she said yes anyways. They headed into the bedroom and like always, he took off his clothes and climbed into bed waiting for her. She knew exactly what was going to happen before it did. She tried for years to get him to loosen up, try new things, but not her Charlie. He squeezed her breast a couple of times, rubbed her clit for a few seconds then climbed on top of her.

"Look at me Charlie, say something nasty to me," Robin purred as she grinded her hips into him.

"Hey, you know I don't like talking during sex. Relax baby and enjoy the ride." Charlie went back to his thrusting. A few moments later, he grunted and then rolled off her. "Like that?" He smiled at her.

Robin just smiled back at him. She watched him get out of the bed, pull on his pants, and head out to the living room. The sound of the TV clicking on grated at her. Nothing was getting through to him. The hints, books, magazine articles, hell coming straight out and telling him none of it worked. Robin was starved for romance, starved for some hot sex.

She picked up her book she had been reading the night before. "Take me away, Barbarian man." She laughed looking at the cover. A well-muscled warrior wearing little to nothing was standing in front of a smaller woman. His sword was drawn, ready to defend his love. Robin opened the book to where she left off and began reading.

A few hours later, she closed the book and stretched out on the bed. The floor under her shook violently. "Charlie!!" she cried out as she huddled in the bed.

"Shhh, calm down woman, a little earth quake nothing more." Charlie climbed into bed with her.

"An earthquake in Ohio?"

"It has happen, see there it is over." Charlie patted her on the hand and climbed out of bed.

A bright light flooded the bedroom. "What the hell…" Charlie said as he covered his eyes. "You stay here." He went to his gun cabinet and grabbed his rifle. "I mean it, Robin, stay here."

"Yes my warrior man." Robin giggled.

"What….never mind, just stay here." Charlie hurried out of the room and headed for the kitchen door. "Damn hunters and their stupid spot lights. Didn't they know that is illegal?" Charlie cursed and mumbled as he put his jacket on. But before he could reach the door it burst into pieces, sending wood shards everywhere.

Charlie gripped his gun and quickly pointed at the door. He fired two shots, whoever broke his door will be paying a high price, he thought. When he opened his eyes, his jaw dropped. Standing before him were four of the largest men he had ever seen. They had large swords and wore only what appear to be loincloths.

"This isn't fucking Halloween." Charlie raised his gun again but before he could fire, the largest of the men knocked the gun from his hand.

"It is but a weaker male," Saa said, grabbing a handful of Charlie's short dark hair. "He doesn't even have his warrior's length."

"My what…." Charlie punched and kicked at the large man but was easily thrown aside as though he weighed as little as a child.

"Mmmm, I smell pussy," Niro growled, standing next to the bedroom door.

"Get the fuck away from there!!" Charlie dragged himself up only to be met by a strong fist, it knocked him out instantly.

"Why didn't we just slay him?" Saa said, breathing in the air. "I want that pussy."

Niro stopped Saa from breaking the door. "I will gather the female, you wait." Niro's hand tightened on the hilt of his sword when he heard Saa's growls.

Niro waited for Saa to back off then rammed open the door. He just stood there as his eyes feasted on the small woman's body.

Robin backed up toward the end of the room, shaking her head in disbelief. She was face to face with a barbarian is the only word that popped into her mind. He was a solid wall of muscle, stood at least six and a half feet tall, his black hair was thick, and hung down the length of his back. His face was the most handsome thing she had ever seen, chiseled features, full lips and dazzling green eyes. He wore only a leather loin cloth, she had to do a second take on that fact, metal wrist bands and had a large knife strap to his thigh.

"I must be dreaming…" Robin backed up even more as the large man moved toward her.

"I am Niro and I mean you know harm," he said his voice deep and velvety.

"Oh look you can speak English how convenient for me, huh. Oh why ain't I waking up?" Robin moved to the other side of the bed.

"Your language was not hard to learn, it is very similar to mine." He walked to her, his cock already becoming hard looking at the little woman. Never had he seen such a delicate looking female. She came up to the middle of his chest, very soft and curvy, large breasts, his eyes couldn't leave her breasts.

His eyes watched her tits bounce in the flimsy cover she had on. He licked his lips wanting to feast on those tits. He forced his eyes to her face. She was very pretty, soft features, blue sparkling eyes and those lips ummm… he hurried to her causing her to step back. He reached for her and threw her over his shoulder. This one was his.

"Put me down!!" Robin pounded on his back.

"You must come with me."

"What have you done with Charlie?" She stopped fighting what was the point she obviously wasn't hurting the big ox.

"Your male is no longer your concern."

"Niro," A deep male's voice boomed in her ear. The next thing Robin felt was someone burying their face in her pussy. She felt a wet, hungry tongue lap and bathe every inch of her pussy.

"Saa, get back to the ship." Niro pushed him away from Robin.

"Mmm, her pussy is sweet." Saa buried his face back into her pussy. Niro pushed him away again and headed into the kitchen. He had to get the female back onto the ship.

"Charlie!" Robin cried out as fear started to take over her.

"Your male will live, but you are coming with me," Niro said, giving her a gentle slap on her ass. He saw the hungry look on Saa's face and knew it was time to leave. Damn it he was going to have to fight Saa for the woman, there was no way around it. He hated fighting his friend but he sure the hell would for this sweet smelling pussy.

Robin felt really hot and saw only white for a few seconds when her eyes adjusted she was inside a metal chamber. What was odd about it was that it looked like a bedroom. She felt the soft furs under her and almost started to laugh. The fur covered bed and weapons hanging around looked terribly out of place in this .... Robin bolted up. "A freaking spaceship!! There is no way....I mean no fucking way." She jumped out of the bed and headed over to the metal door. She looked everywhere for the switch. "Damn it! There is always some kind of button or something in the movies."

The sound of swords clashing caught her attention. She pressed her ear against the door. The sound of metal and men grunting was all she could hear. Then it stopped. She pressed herself closer against the door straining to hear. The next thing she knew she was on the floor face down.

"What are you doing?" Niro said. He was a bit shocked when she fell out of the door when he opened it. He licked his lips seeing her bare ass exposed to him, nice and round, just liked he preferred.

Robin quickly pulled her robe down over her ass and stood up. All she could see was a wall of muscle before her. The smell of man invaded her nose causing her pussy to dampen. "Where are you taking me?" She walked back into the room.

"Malka." Niro's eyes drank in all of her. His cock so hard, it ached. There was no way he was going to keep his promise. He had just fought Saa for the right to choose which of the two females he wanted to have. He decided on this dark haired beauty.

Robin looked up at Niro she could see the hunger in his eyes. Her eyes drifted down to his leather loincloth. Oh yeah he was thinking what she thought he was thinking. His cock had to be enormous to create such an impressive bulge.

"Stay away from me." Robin climbed on the bed and huddled in the corner. Everything began to sink in. She was in what appeared to be a spaceship and was headed for somewhere called Malka. Her eyes darted up and down Niro's large frame. This impressive wall of muscles could do whatever he wanted to her and she would be powerless to stop it. Fear, confusion and a real doubt of her own sanity engulfed her.

Niro saw the fear in her face. He would be rattled too if someone plucked him off his planet and whisked him away to another. He carefully sat down on the bed and tried to ignore his painful erection. "It will be alright," he said in a quiet voice. "I will not hurt you." He petted her lightly. Her hair, a rich brown color that hung down to her shoulders, felt so soft in his hands. "You will like Malka." He didn't know what to say or what to do to ease her fear.

Robin looked up into his dazzling green eyes; the gentleness in them was soothing in a strange way. "Why me, why take me?"

"You were the first female of child bearing age we came across." Niro was fighting hard not to ravish her. He wanted to bury his cock deep inside her warm, wet pussy.

"Oh lucky me, can't win the lottery but I am chosen for this." She started to cry this can't be real, it just can't.

"No, No, don't do that." Niro gently wiped away the falling tears. He groaned softly when Robin wrapped her arms around him seeking some kind of comfort. He placed his arms around her and just enjoyed the softness and warmth of her body. He could feel her tears dampen his chest. "Don't cry, it pains me to see a female crying."

"I am sorry I shouldn't have done that. I mean I don't even know you." Robin couldn't take her eyes off his full lips.

"I will leave you alone now. You probably need time to think." Niro couldn't control himself much longer. But he wouldn't allow himself to ravish this frighten woman, not now anyways.

"Thank you Niro."

Hearing his name coming from her lips almost caused him to lose the little control he had left. "What is your name?" he asked.

"Robin," she replied quietly.

"Robin." He bowed his head and left quickly before he changed his mind and fucked the hell out of her right now.

Protector of My Heart is available in Ebook and Print now

Justus Roux's Erotic Tales
Where Love and Erotica Know No Boundaries

Sizzling sample chapters of all of Justus Roux's novels, short Stories written by Justus Roux and a variety of talented Guest writers and poets, a monthly contest to win books, all of this awaits you at <u>*www.justusroux.com*</u>

May 2005
"Who's Your Daddy?"

There is nothing quite as sexy as an alpha male. Come on, you know it's true. This anthology contains twenty-one of the hottest short stories paying homage to this sexy breed of man. Whether you want to be the alpha male or be loved by him there is a story in here for you. Warriors, lovers, husbands, business men, Masters, oh the list goes on.

An ensemble of talented writers of erotica will tantalize you with their sizzling tales of the alpha male. Enjoy!

Justus Roux's Master Series

Each book explores the world of Master and Slaves.

My Master- the first book in the series introduces you to Master Drake. He is known as the Master of Pleasure. He knows what will bring his pets and guest the most pleasure. But he wasn't expecting to fall in love with Jessica Scott, a woman trick to come to his island by her husband.

Master's Ecstasy- You explore Master Drake's world more and learn about his pets, especially his favorite pet Ecstasy. Plus you are introduced to Master Dante; he is dubbed the Master of Pain.

Obey!- Delve into Master Dante's world with Anna and Tom, a married couple who have no idea just want they are in for. See Master Dante's many sides as he trains this married couple.

Sweet Rapture- Rapture is Master Drake's most trusted pet. But he is unprepared for Alexandra and falls for her right away. Alexandra is frightened of Rapture's world though she can't deny her attraction to him.

Mistress Angelique- She is Master Dante's Mistress, the only woman Dante will every love and the only woman he has ever trained.

Explore her castle with Brent as he tries to free his brother from Master Dante.

*   **Wrath's Lust**- Wrath once the slave of Master Dante, now the pet of Master Drake, he is caught in a vortex of emotions when he realizes his need for Lust. She is another one of Master Drake's pet, but she finds herself wanting to only belong to Wrath.*

*   **Breathless**- This anthology contains the novella Master Drake and introduces the reader to Master Nikolai. He has asked Drake to help train his favorite slave Jade. However Drake is trying to heal from the lost of three of his pets.*

*   Plus on Justus Roux's website follow Jade's training and learn more about Master Nikolai in a series of short stories. A new one is posted at the beginning of every month.*

*   Discover Justus Roux's Master series and explore love and erotica without boundaries.*
*   All books available now.*

Printed in the United Kingdom
by Lightning Source UK Ltd.
123570UK00001B/34/A